"Speaking OUT"

KEN HANES

Three Rivers Press/New York

A complete list of credits appears on pages 190–192.

Published by Three Rivers Press, 201 East 50th Street, New York, New York 10022.
Member of the Crown Publishing Group.
Random House, Inc. New York, Toronto, London, Sydney, Auckland
www.randomhouse.com

THREE RIVERS PRESS is a trademark of Crown Publishers, Inc.

Printed in the United States of America

Design by Lynne Amft

Library of Congress Cataloging-in-Publication Data
Hanes, Ken. Speaking out / Ken Hanes.—1st ed.
1. Gays—Quotations. I. Title.
PN6084.G35H37 1998
306.76'6—dc21 97-44919

ISBN 0-517-88791-6

1 3 5 7 9 10 8 6 4 2

First Edition

Introduction

Each January, I perform a beginning-of-the-year ritual: Paging through my outgoing day planner, I highlight the names and phone numbers hastily scribbled in the corners and margins of the schedules that were my last year's life. After deciding which numbers to keep, I type them up and then attach the orderly list to my new calendar.

This year, as I was glancing over the names freshly added to my phone list, I had a realization: Most of the gay men on the list were quite remarkable people, and most of the truly remarkable people on the list were gay men. Although I imagine this phenomenon says more about me and my circle of friends than about any larger pattern, I mentioned my experience to non-gay-male friends, and many (though certainly not all) had had similar experiences. Which leads to an odd question: The people bursting with humanity and goodness, the ones who make you happy, well, just by being on the planet—why are a seemingly inordinate number of these folk gay men?

I've heard people suggest a spiritual explanation—that gays and lesbians are an incarnation of a special spirit, even a third gender, and that it's the queer's role to save the world.

I've heard some say it's genetic—that whatever blend of DNA makes one queer also brews a unique cocktail of extreme sensitivity, talent, and wisdom.

I've heard the belief that it's cultural—that because society dumps a bucket of nasty crap on queers, you either get buried in it or you climb to the top, surviving and blossoming into a stronger, more self-actualized human being.

And then there's the Big A reasoning—that the previously unfathomable hardship of AIDS has stimulated a profound transformation, catapulting queers—gay men, of course, particularly—into new ways of thinking and being.

All of the above sound plausible to me, but who knows? I don't pretend to have an answer. But whatever the reason, the gifts gay men have to offer one another are vast and profound. The collective lessons of the collective community are astonishing. Wisdom abounds. Caring soars. Humor blooms in unlikely places.

I'm not so naive to believe that all gay men are splendid specimens of humanity. I've met more than my share of gay men so relentlessly battered and bruised by the world that their humanity has evaporated into thin air. But by the tone of this introduction, it should be unambiguously clear that this book focuses on the plentiful riches that gay men have to offer one another. *Speaking Out* is intended to be a celebration.

In these pages, hundreds of gay men share their thoughts and feelings about [illegible] and loving. Because there's no consensus in the gay community about much of anything, I don't expect anyone who reads *Speaking Out* to agree with all the ruminations included here. I certainly don't. Some of the material is even contradictory, since the different men in this volume don't share the same hearts and brains. *Speaking Out* will most likely present some ideas with which you'll wholeheartedly agree, just as it is likely to offer ideas with which you'll strongly disagree. Yet these divergences and contradictions are the point. With material from gay men across our society, *Speaking Out,* I hope, reflects the amazing breadth of attitudes and beliefs of gay men across America.

“Brotherhood”

Accept Yourself as a Link in a Chain

I am not a beginning.

I am not an end.

I am a link in a chain.

The strength of which depends on my own contributions, as well as the contributions of those before and after me. . . . When I am aware of this unity, and refuse to let my self-doubt and lack of self-confidence interfere, it is one of the most wonderful feelings I've ever experienced. I am a necessary part of an important search to which there is no end.

—KEITH HARING
Artist

Our unhappiness as scared queer children doesn't only isolate us, it also politicizes us. It inculcates in us a desire for connection that is all the stronger because we have experienced its absence. Our suffering teaches us solidarity; or it should.

—TONY KUSHNER
Playwright

I know lots of queers think that rainbow flags and pink triangles are cliché and overused. But when I visit another city and I see a flag hanging on someone's porch, or a bumper sticker, I find it very comforting. It makes me feel more at home. I display my rainbow flag as a banner, a warm welcome flag for other gay folks. It's not for the aesthetics. It's for the community.

—NOAH FRANKLIN
Artist

Give Back to Your Community

To really be a gay or lesbian citizen, you must also give back to your community. You have to reach out and help it.

—PAUL MONETTE
Writer

I have tried to internalize what I have learned from my patients. I remember how they have endured and how they have taught me what I once thought was impossible, something I thought I might never learn: the limitless ways that I can give back to many communities.

—RAFAEL CAMPO
Doctor

Stop Attacking One Another

We have the T-shirts beating up on the suits, and the suits beating up on the T-shirts. ACT UP beating up on Queer Nation, and Queer Nation beating up on ACT UP. ACT UP beating up on AIDS Project Los Angeles, and AIDS Project Los Angeles beating up on ACT UP. ACT UP beating up on people of color, and people of color beating up on ACT UP. ACT UP beating up on its own members, and its own members beating up on ACT UP. ACT UP beating up on everyone else, and everyone else beating up on ACT UP.

There is this tremendous anger, this insidious anger, this internecine anger, eating us up, chewing our innards, and drying out our souls.

If we don't get our act together fast, we are going to do ourselves in, far faster than we could ever give credit to AIDS.

—KIM SINGH
Activist

When you're oppressed you feel powerless to attack other people, so you start attacking people like yourself. It's really a tragedy because nothing is ever going to get done as long as we tear each other up.

—CLYDE HALL

Attorney/Magistrate

Be a Role Model

Older men, listen up: When you were growing up and coming out, times were more oppressive and secretive. AIDS had not yet made us as public as we are today. In that time, you did not have the benefit of gay mentors and role models. It was not possible. Today, my generation lacks gay mentors and role models. Those few that we have are rich, white stars or HIV-positive. Be our mentors. Don't fuck us. Teach us.

—ROBERT HOLZMEIER
Queer Activist

One obligation—and potential joy—of being out is being a role model and ambassador.

—RODNEY SIMARD
Associate Professor of English

As a public figure, I think I have a responsibility to present images that break down boundaries and stereotypes.

—ANTHONY RAPP
Actor

I hate that gay role models are supposed to be just like straight people. As if straight people were even like that.

—PAUL RUDNICK
Writer (from Jeffrey*)*

The elderly can demonstrate to those younger and dispirited that they can live long, happy, healthy lives. By becoming models for the value of longevity and love, they can show that aging as a gay man does not destroy the capacity for relationships or intimacy.

—RICHARD A. ISAY
Psychiatrist

Find Some Role Models

If you have neither sympathetic pals nor guardian angels, find congenial gurus wherever you can. My earliest ones were Oz, Mother Goose, and Buster Keaton. Later I added Shakespeare, Zen, and Stravinsky. —JAMES BROUGHTON

Writer/Filmmaker/Poet

A role model doesn't have to be gay. When I am in a tough, gay-specific situation, and I'm not sure what to do, I ask myself what Gandhi would have done if he'd been gay.

—DEAN MATSUMOTO

Searcher

I spent most of my life searching for a role model. But in the past year or two, I've realized that my life has been about becoming my own role model.

—TONY ZIMBARDI

Activist

Learn Your History

It's important for younger queers to learn our history. Get in touch with your roots. I have lots of respect for the older generation of queers and what they've been through. When things are tough, I think of them and know I shouldn't bitch so much.

—NAME WITHHELD

The only way we'll have real pride is when we demand recognition of a culture that isn't just sexual. It's all there. All through history, we've been there, but we have to claim it, and identify who was in it, and articulate what's in our minds and hearts and all our creative contributions to this earth.

—LARRY KRAMER

Writer/Activist (from The Normal Heart*)*

Gay men and lesbians have a history as old as the world because we've been here that long. But do we ever hear about it from the majority culture? Almost never!

For years, they tried to hide our very existence from us! For how many generations did most gay men grow up thinking they were the only ones who felt desire for other men? The homophobes don't want us to know our history, because a people without history has no power. If a young gay man comes of age aware of all the brilliant gay men who have graced this planet, aware of all their astonishing accomplishments, then self-hate and the closet begin to seem pretty silly. Once a gay man understands how deep our roots go, how could he possibly think there's something wrong or unnatural about his sexuality?

We have to seek out and actively educate ourselves about our history. That's how we'll grow both as individuals and as a culture.

—MARTIN LEVINSON
Educator

Reasons to Come Out

Being out is the key to everything. If you feel shame about being gay, how can you feel good about anything else in your life?

—KEVYN AUCOIN
Makeup Artist

Coming out may be difficult and stressful at times, but it is a rebirth. You are at the very beginning of a new life, one in which you will, for the first time in a very long time, be able to live in freedom, honesty, and pride.

—MICHELANGELO SIGNORILE
Writer

Until you are out, you won't know what happiness is. —IAN McKELLEN
Actor

A lot of people are not homophobic, but they think they're supposed to be. They think that if they don't express prejudice, people will think there's something the matter with them. . . . When you come out, you give straight people the chance to learn that it's okay to not be prejudiced. —BARNEY FRANK
U.S. Representative

The more up-front you are about your sexuality, the more you'll be accepted by quality people. —JASON PLOURDE
Social Worker

Understand that coming out is a *strategy* for self-acceptance, not its equivalent.

—MARTIN DUBERMAN
Writer/Historian

By coming out, gay people serve to inspire, educate, and inform gay and nongay Americans by presenting the true diversity of the gay community. It is up to us to let the world know the truth about who we are.

—HUMAN RIGHTS CAMPAIGN
"COMING OUT DAY" POSTER

Coming out leads to living out. To make a difference in the course of justice, our own lives or anyone else's, we must come out *and* live out.

—JAMES ROBISCOE
Novelist

The Other Side: Not Coming Out

When asked, "Shall I tell my mother I'm gay?" I reply "Never tell your mother *anything*."

—QUENTIN CRISP
Actor/Writer

I see no reason to come out unless it's important to your work or your politics. . . . There's this new attitude that you're either out or you're a bad guy. That's ridiculous. There's no personal choice in that kind of thinking.

—FARLEY GRANGER
Actor

There are valid reasons not to come out. Maybe you're living with your parents, and dependent on them for your basic needs. Maybe you'd lose your job. Maybe you'd be in physical danger. Sure, coming out is probably healthier psychologically. But if you're going to be in physical danger, if you're going to be kicked out of your home, then psychological health isn't going to save your life.

—BRADLEY CRANE
Interior Designer

Understand That the Closet Hurts

Keeping secrets about your sexuality is the most dangerous and potentially harmful thing that one can do, because I think it separates you from the truth and from your family, which is a big price to pay.

—SANDY GALLIN
Manager/Producer

If you stay in the closet, you don't get what you deserve. You get the raw deal.

—IAN McKELLEN
Actor

You must come out. Come out to your parents. I know it is hard and will hurt them, but think about how they will hurt you in the voting booth. Come out to your relatives. I know that is hard and will upset them, but think of how they will hurt you in the voting booth. Come out to your friends, if they are indeed your friends. Come out to your neighbors, to your fellow workers, to the people who work where you eat and shop. Come out only to the people you know and who know you. Not to anyone else. But once and for all, break down the myths, destroy the lies and distortions. For your sake. For their sake. There will be no safe "closet" for any gay person. So break out of yours today—tear the damn thing down once and for all! —HARVEY MILK

Hero and Martyr

Getting Healthy

For too long, we gay men have been told we're bad, sinful, and immoral. These words hurt us, constantly chipping away at our self-esteem. Then low self-esteem leads some gay men to self-destructive behavior—that is, to sleep around without using condoms or to look to find love for ourselves in other people's eyes. We must learn to defend ourselves from these words, to love ourselves for who we are. We have to realize we exist as whole and separate individuals worthy of another's admiration and love. Only then will our relationships have the ability to last forever.

—STEVEN MANSON
Ph.D. Candidate in Economics

To love oneself is the beginning of a life-long romance. —OSCAR WILDE
Writer

In 1984, at age forty, I began opening the closet door. Letting others know was surprisingly easy. But getting over my own homophobia was not simple. The old negativity kept eating my self-esteem. My confidence would come and go like a radio signal that was clear and strong one minute and fuzzy and weak the next. It's taken me a decade to get over my own homophobia. How have I done it? Friends. Venturing out. I began noticing my gay friends being okay with themselves. I bathed in their acceptance until it wore off on me.

—DEE LEAHMAN
Mediator

Gays often go through their adolescence later than others. Don't delay your adolescence. Get it over with. It's no easier in your forties than in your teens.

—NATE BAILEY
Forty-Three-Year-Old Adolescent

A man should be more than an aggressive mind with an embarrassed cock attached. A man who fails to develop compassion and tolerance is not completely human.

—JAMES BROUGHTON
Writer/Filmmaker/Poet

If you're gay, get a gay therapist. You'll communicate better, you'll bond better, and when you do role-playing, sometimes you'll get to be Keanu Reeves.

—ROMAN HANS
Writer

We have struggled to create new relationships and families to replace traditional heterosexual ones. Could we create a new model for relating to one another that is based on frankness and honesty? We've been reminded in the most painful ways of just how precious is the time we have to spend with another person. Can we afford to waste any of that time with dishonesty?

—HENRY E. SCOTT
Media Consultant/Writer

Create Healthy Social Settings

I strongly believe that one of the most important things any of us can do for the long-term well-being of the gay community is to create healthy gay social settings. So much of our social culture nowadays is centered on bars, clubs, and partying. This leads too many men into the trap of overusing drugs and alcohol, and it often leaves those who don't choose those avenues isolated and alone.

We need to work so that every city and town in this country has gay community centers, gay coffeehouses, gay boys and girls clubs, gay support centers, and so on, so that all gay and lesbian youth have healthy, affirming alternatives for their emergence into adult gay life.

—CLYDE THOMASEN
Teacher

Set up some boys and girls clubs so we have places to go. It's not like we can do it ourselves.

—MICHAEL L.
Sixteen Years Old

Please, Help Kids

Please, help kids. Don't let kids kill themselves because they're gay. They think about doing it. They really do. Find them, because they can't find you. Find them, and help them. Please.

—NAME WITHHELD BY REQUEST
(a seventeen-year-old high school student)

As gay, lesbian, bisexual, and transgendered youth come under more and more scrutiny, as suicides and homelessness continue to rise . . . the adult gay community should be doing all it can to make the world a better place for its youth.

—WILSON CRUZ
Actor

Those of us who made it safely through our youth owe it to them to do all we can, not only at election time but also throughout the year, to help make every American town and school a place where they can thrive in openness, dignity, and integrity.

—BRUCE BAWER
Writer

We have a huge obligation not only to fight against homophobia in the adult world, hoping that will trickle down to gay kids, but also to fight just as hard against the major problems that confront gay youth, especially their lack of belief in the future.

—GABRIEL ROTELLO
Writer

Light Another Flame

What I know now is that people are extraordinarily cruel. What I know now is that seemingly ordinary people are often extraordinary. What I know now is that I am a changed person because of AIDS. I am angrier, sadder, a bit tougher. I am also inspired, sometimes hopeful, and at times even amazed. What I know now is that one flame lights another, which lights another, which lights another, which lights another.

—COREY ROSKIN
Activist

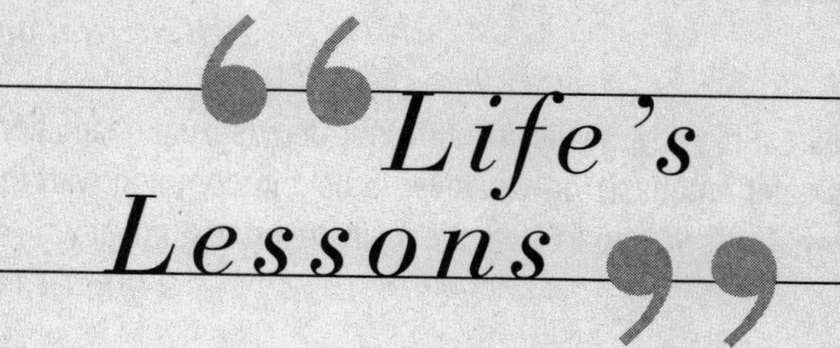

"*Life's Lessons*"

Elders Speak

Live in your body, not your mind. Eat more chocolate than beans. Fuck often. Follow your bliss over hill and dale. . . . Watch out for conformity. Middle-class morality is ever ready to kidnap you.

—JAMES BROUGHTON
Writer/Filmmaker/Poet

Move to the nearest big city, neither confirm nor deny sexual orientation, and above all, try to lay greater emphasis on whatever is held in common with the rest of the world than on what sets you apart from the mainstream of humanity.

—QUENTIN CRISP
Actor/Writer

If someone leads you to feel weak or confused, do not trust him with your life, your body, or your time.

—MALCOLM McKAY
Erotic Activist

The secret of happiness is to open your arms to all, for there is some good in every individual. If you do this, you can never be bored. You learn the frailties of people and try to stir them up, making them laugh and instilling them with a certain optimism, which so many people lack.

—DAVID HERBERT
Writer/Aristocrat/Partygiver

Being gay for me means gentleness, sensitivity, warmth, and service to others. When I meet a gay person who is the opposite of those things, I am offended. Because that's someone who has not realized himself or herself.

—MALCOLM BOYD
Author/Activist/Clergyman

I came out at age fifty-six. It's never too late. Even though being a kid, a teenager, a young adult, and an adult gay man in one year's time has been nothing short of wonderful, I regret waiting so long. Don't wait. —NICHOLAS MERCURY

Information Specialist

To those of you who still hide, I say come out. There is no reason whatsoever to stay in that stifling closet any longer. Leave the shadows and come out into the light. You will find that you will be welcomed, not only by your brothers and sisters but by all whom you love if they are worthy of your love. —MARVIN LIEBMAN

Gay Activist (who came out when he was sixty-seven years old)

Young Men Speak

Yes, I'm young. Yes, I'm cute. But I'm not a boy toy. I'm not a twinkie. I have a fully functional brain, and I use it. Don't condescend to me because of my youth.

—ZACHARY DAVIS
Student

If you are into sex with boys who are underage, don't call yourself gay. Call yourself a child molester, because that's what you are. It disgusts me. You make me ashamed to be gay.

—NAME WITHHELD

Accept that I might want your friendship, your advice, and your mentorship without wanting you to fuck me. And don't take that as an insult.

—JOHN SOLBERG
Label-Free

Stop talking about the good old days. I am sick of hearing about how blissful your life was before AIDS. Those of us who had no gay life pre-AIDS—we don't want to hear it.

—EDWARD ARLISS
Student

Stop using cross-gender pronouns. I'm a boy, and I like being a boy. I am not a "she," so don't call me "she."

—CHRISTOPHER COULTER
Still Growing

Teach me how to set limits and respect boundaries, not how to suck cock.

—MARK
Twenty-One Years Old

When in doubt, ask a lesbian.

—DEMOSTHENES PANAYOTOU
International Environmental Specialist

I've been mostly on the streets for the past few years. I meet older guys all the time. This one guy, in his seventies, he gave me a place to stay—no strings attached, he said. I needed fifty dollars to buy some magic cards. He said he'd give me the money, but he needed collateral. So I gave him my skateboard. I couldn't give him the fifty bucks back. Where am I going to get fifty dollars? So then he tried to force me to be a, you know, a queen. I said, "I've been there, and it bites. Leave me alone." He kept trying, so I said, "Leave me alone or I'll charge you with harassment." I left. He still has my skateboard.

Now older guys still try to pick me up, and I wish I could kick every one of their asses. What I've learned is this: There's always strings attached. If a guy's more than twice my age, I stay away!

—BRIAN
Sixteen-Year-Old Bi-Boy

I was eighteen years old, living at home. My mom didn't know. I had a gay friend. At first, when he'd call me, my mom said he sounded funny over the phone. Then he sent me a card. I wasn't home when the mail arrived. My mom pressed down the envelope against the card, and she could make out the image of two guys arm in arm.

It wasn't even a graphic card or anything, just two guys being affectionate. But she opened the envelope—and, well, then she knew.

She called me at work. "You're coming home after work, aren't you?" she asked. Actually, it was more like "You're coming home [sniff, sniff] after work [sniff, sniff], aren't you?"

I instantly knew she knew. It was a sixth sense. So I went home after work. Oh, did I mention Mom was—is—a fundamentalist Christian? She told me, "God has different plans for you. We'll get you help."

Then she barely said a word to me until two weeks later, when she kicked me out of the house. She said, "I have another son I'm trying to raise here. Have all of your stuff out by Saturday." That was that. I was eighteen years old and out on my own.

I hadn't planned on coming out, because I knew all this would happen. But my not planning on it didn't stop it from happening. If you live with parents who are going to reject you, you've got to prepare. Don't just wait for it to happen. Take control and prepare.

—NAME WITHHELD

Irreverent Men Speak

One should always be wary of anyone who promises that their love will last longer than a weekend.

—QUENTIN CRISP
Actor/Writer

Never vow to remain friends forever.

—JAMES CARROLL PICKET
Writer

Girls' names for boys are permissible only in bars after midnight when you're very drunk.

—DAVID LOOVIS
Writer

Don't read Bible passages to him during an erection.

—ERIC RAPTOSH
Pianist

Ask before you tie him up.

—DAVID B. FEINBERG
Writer (from Eighty-Sixed*)*

The way to keep some of your time to yourself is to maintain yourself so unattractively that nobody else is interested in any of it.

—ANDY WARHOL
Artist

Don't accept an invitation to a toga party.

—JEARL NEWMAN
Nurse

Don't Make Such a Big Deal About Penises

Just because he can't serve you breakfast with a cup of coffee in one hand and a glass of juice in the other, and still hold a dozen doughnuts—so what? Can't you use a plate for the doughnuts like everyone else? Set your priorities.

—DAVID ALLISON
Non–Size Queen

Penises are fun but not intelligent. They have no I.Q. Penises are cute, but they're not logical. Don't let them make decisions for you.

—RON ROMANOVSKY AND PAUL PHILLIPS
Singers/Songwriters

Remember, it's not the size of his urethra that counts, but the size of the heart that pumps blood to it.

—TOM REESER
Heartiologist

Don't Be a Bitch

Bitchiness and wit are *not* the same. In any case, cultivate the most valuable verbal abilities: appropriate and sincere compliments and apologies.

—RODNEY SIMARD
Associate Professor of English

I try not to be an evil queen, but sometimes you have to.

—BOY GEORGE
Singer

Remember, when you tear someone to shreds, it hurts. Try to remember the time in history when you didn't feel like you fit in.

—RICHARD BREDON
Counselor for the Deaf

These gay men who think it's high art to channel Oscar Wilde or Bette Davis or some *Melrose Place* diva or any one of the hundreds of icons of bitchiness our culture offers—so many gay men think that in the name of wit, if the result is a laugh, it's okay for them to lacerate others with their verbal swords simply because they possess the ability. No! Bitchiness hurts. Let's stop it. —TOBIAS ALDRICH

Customer Service Representative

Attitude

Lose it. —AARON M., ADAM O., AL T., ALEXANDER W., ALLEN J., ANDREW K., ANDY S., BARRY T., BILL P., BOB L., BOB R., BOB S., BRAD L., BRADLEY A., BRENT P., BRYAN B., CAL T., CARL C., CARLOS S., CASEY M., CHAD P., CHARLES L., CHRIS Y., CHRISTOPHER O., CHUCK E., CLEVELAND F., CLIFF H., CODY W., COREY A., CRAIG I., DALE K., DAN U., DANIEL J., DARRYL C., DAVE G., DAVE Y., DAVID B., DAVID H., DAVID U., DEAN T., DEN P., DENNIS J., DENNIS R., DEV G., DILAN N., DON F., DOUGLAS T., DOUGLASS B., DUSTIN S., DWIGHT S., DWAYNE G., DYLAN K., EDWARD R., ERIC C., ERIC N., ERIC W., ETHAN R., EVAN I., FLYNN M., FRANK T., FRANK Y., GARY B., GARY L., GIL P., GLENN F., GRADY H., GREG J., GREGORY D., HANS S., HART D., HAYES A., HENRY J., HOWE K., HUGH R., IAN F., IAN J., JAKE G., JAMES G., JAMES H., JAMES T., JAMES W., JASON L., JASON W., JAY T., JED H., JEFF P., JEFF Z., JEFFREY D., JEFFREY M., JERRY C., JESS F., JIMMY V., JOEL R., JOHN F., JONATHAN A., JONATHAN G., JONATHAN P., JORDAN R., JOSÉ Q., JOSEPH O., JOSH G., JUSTIN I., KEN D., KENNETH Y., KEVIN T., KEVIN W., KIRK O., KYLE H., LANE S., LARRY U., LARRY W., LEE T., LES K., LUCAS D., LYLE R., MARC R., MARK C., MARK N., MARK P., MARTIN H., MATTHEW M.,

MICHAEL C., MICHAEL F., MICHAEL L., MICHAEL R., MIKE D., MIKE G., MIKE W., MILES R., NATHAN B., NICHOLAS E., PARKER B., PATRICK C., PATRICK D., PETER V., PHIL G., PHILIP Y., QUENTIN H., RAFAEL R., RALPH Z., RANDY F., REED P., RICH T., RICHARD A., RICHARD J., RICHARD O., ROBERT B., ROBERT J., ROBERT Y., ROD K., ROGER S., ROGER T., RONNIE R., RYAN D., SAM W., SEAN K., SID H., STEPHAN F., STEVE G., STEVE M., STEVEN C., STEVEN L., TAD N., TAYLOR D., TED G., THOMAS P., TIMOTHY D., TOM K., TONY S., TRAVIS A., VINCENT R., WADE R., WALT F., WARREN G., WESLEY H., WILLIAM A., WILLIAM J., WILLIAM W., ZACHARY P.

More on Attitude

Attitude without substance is just plain bitterness.

—MARK DAVIS
(as Peter Eisenhower Westchester III) Comic

Most guys affect attitude because they think it's attractive. But attitude is *never* attractive. Get over it. Work on your own insecurities instead.

—MITCHELL GAYNOR
Gardener

Gay men having attitude and being unfriendly is my pet peeve. But so many gay men overstep the line between friendly flirting and aggressively coming on to someone who doesn't want to be come on to. A lot of guys use attitude as a self-defense against overly aggressive types. If you don't like others' attitude, ask yourself how many times have you come on so strong that it's made someone's attitude go up?

—PATRICK BROWNE
Doctor and Film Critic

Be Authentic

Find your voice. Whether it's deep or high doesn't matter; being authentic does.

—MICHAEL KEARNS
Actor

I hate it when guys try to be more than what they really are. Just be yourself, because that's the guy I want to fall in love with, not some image you've put on to impress.

—GRAHAM WATTS
Locksmith

I have promised myself that I will not remain silent, invisible, unknown. The choice for me is not whether or not I am a gay man, but whether or not I am honest about who I am with myself and others.

—E. OTIS CHARLES
Retired Episcopal Bishop

As children, we probably learned or feared that telling the truth about who we were would get us in trouble—made fun of at school, maybe even kicked out of our homes. When we were younger, lying and not communicating were necessary survival techniques. But as adults, these techniques are destructive. They stop us from leading full, honest lives and having successful relationships. Learning to tell the truth is crucial to making our lives and relationships work. —ANTHONY HELLMAN

Recovering Liar

Living with HIV or AIDS

Protease inhibitors have changed my life, as they've changed many, many other people's lives. My life has new possibilities now. I think of the future with optimism. But I'm trying very hard not to get caught up in any euphoria. I want to be realistic. Who knows how long my renewed health will last? The floor could fall out tomorrow. Yet, at the same time, I don't want to worry about tomorrow so much that it ruins my today. There's a balance.

—DOUGLAS MINOT
Flight Attendant

Living with AIDS has always been extraordinarily difficult, and with the dawn of protease inhibitors it's gotten even more difficult for me. The miracle drugs—they don't work for me. I can't tolerate them. Yet I watch most of my friends with AIDS respond well to them. I see renewed health and vitality all around me. Now I have to cope not only with AIDS but with the psychological pain of feeling abandoned. For many, many people, for whatever reasons, the protease inhibitors don't work. For us, the AIDS crisis is still a crisis. Don't forget us. Don't let us slip through the cracks.

—EVAN HOWARD
Former Lifeguard

We must find paths that allow survival not only as human organisms, but as communities of *human beings,* regardless of serostatus, who are able to live passionately and intimately, to love, and to make lives in other regards worth living. Survival, in this sense, has nothing to do with our antibody status, and nothing to do with how much time we have on the planet—it has only to do with how much *heart* we are able to discover within ourselves and bring to our daily lives.

—WALT ODETS
Writer/Psychologist

Laughing in the Face of AIDS

As Dame Edna says, take your vitamin L every day. Laughter. Life without laughter is unbearable, and that's even more true when you have AIDS. Laughter makes the unbearable more bearable.

—GARRETT JASPERS
Grande Dame in Training

It's been the general rule that you don't use wit in the face of tragedy because it might trivialize it. That's crazy. It's especially important at those times. You acknowledge the awfulness. I mean, it's not "Oh, AIDS, la-de-da." But you don't let the disease rule. If you do, then it wins.

—PAUL RUDNICK
Writer

Five years and six months after my diagnosis, I'm still around being ornery and getting in people's faces. And I've been in the hospital only twice since I was diagnosed. I attribute my continued good health to being an activist. Activists live longer because we have a fighting spirit, and a fighting spirit is good for the immune system. We tend to think of success mostly in terms of changes of bureaucracy—but maybe success is just one of us sick queens sticking around another week.

—WADE RICHARDS
AIDS Activist

Living Without HIV

I'm so tired of people telling me that because I'm HIV-negative I should count my blessings, don't complain, everything should be okay. Well, no. After fifteen years of burying my friends, having lovers die, seeing friend after friend waste away, *I am not okay,* and God damn it, don't tell me to count my lucky stars.

—SKYLAR SHANNON
Violinist

I am an HIV-negative gay man. And I am invested in remaining negative. Know that my rejection of HIV is not a rejection of you as an HIV-positive man. I can reject HIV, hate HIV, without rejecting or hating you. Please do not be threatened by my HIV-negative status.

—ELIOT SCOTSMAN
Pilot

We say, "I'm HIV-negative." But do people say, "I'm cancer-negative," or "I'm hypertension-negative"? Why would those of us who are free of HIV define ourselves by something we don't have? Don't take on the identity of HIV.

—SHANE BRADLEY
Costumer

Lighten Up and Let It Shine

We don't call ourselves gay for nothing, so lighten up and don't hide your light under a bushel.

—MARTIN WIECH
Hairstylist, Masseur, Practitioner, Writer, and Much, Much More

Tolerance and acceptance are not enough for me—it's celebration I'm aiming for.

—KEVYN AUCOIN
Makeup Artist

Remember, next to your penis or vagina, a positive attitude is your best friend. Good manners and a positive attitude go hand in hand. Conduct yourself with grace and politeness.

—DAVID B. FEINBERG
Writer

“Living in a Hetero World”

Be an Ambassador

I see every heterosexual person I meet as an opportunity to teach someone about tolerance. For example (this really happened), let's say I take a plane trip and get stuck next to some loud-mouthed hick who thinks it's his duty to make sure I understand the difference between a bull, a steer, and an ox. I could bury myself in the in-flight magazine, put up an emotional wall so I don't have to talk to him, change my seat, whatever.

But instead, I talk to him. It may be the first time this man has ever knowingly had a conversation with a gay person. I don't start talking about my favorite anal toys or show him my new piercings, but I casually let him know about my sexuality. Maybe having a nonthreatening encounter will plant a seed of tolerance or acceptance in this guy's mind. And most of us have opportunities like this all the time. It's up to us to present ourselves to the world in a way that allows acceptance.

—JOHN ALBERS
Computer Programmer

I don't understand those parts of the gay community that go out of their way to provoke and anger the straight world. You know, staging kiss-ins, wearing outrageous clothing, throwing condoms, whatever. I see myself as an ambassador. Every interaction I have with someone from the straight community, I see myself as representing my entire community. And I gauge my behavior accordingly.

—JESS JOHNSON
Nurse

Let your light shine before men, that they may see your good works.

—MATTHEW 5:16

There's a lot of discrimination against gays that is based on ignorance of who we are, what we are, what homosexuals do in the world. That's to some extent our fault, because we don't let others know what we accomplish as citizens of this world. That's not right. People should be more forthright about themselves and be ambassadors of their community.

—SIMON LEVAY
Scientist/Writer

Open a Closed Mind

Take a straight friend to a gay bar. A closed mind is a wonderful thing to lose.

—SHANE ALLISON
Living-Room Poet

Educate straight people. When family or old friends don't seem to do the obvious, such as ask about our dating lives, we often assume they're rejecting us because we're gay. However, it's often because they need some education, like "Hey, you ask about Sis's husband but not about my boyfriend. I'd like you to ask about him." That often works wonders.

—MARK C. MICHAEL
Clinical Psychologist and Alpine Hiking Guide

I mention my sexuality in a matter-of-fact way to one stranger a day, usually after they tell me about their girlfriend or boyfriend.

—LARRY ALDRICH
Happy-Go-Lucky Pedestrian

The political value of demonstrating that "we are everywhere" is unmistakable; the more "straight" people become accustomed to the ordinary presence of "queer" people, the less likely they will be to hold bigoted attitudes toward them.

—FRANK BROWNING
Writer

Don't Force Your Sexuality on Anyone

Some people don't want to see my gayness. I can wear my I CAN'T EVEN THINK STRAIGHT T-shirt, have a rainbow flag on my car and a pink triangle button on my backpack, and some people still won't see me as gay. People with blinders are blind. It's not my job to force their eyes open. I just go about living my life honestly. If people don't want to see me, they don't. I'm not going to force-feed anyone my sexuality.

—SLOAN CONNELLY
Computer Programmer

So much of society hears only the "sexual" in the word "homosexual"; they become stuck on their own sexual hang-ups in relating to us. We need to be completely out about our gay nonsexual lives so people can get over thinking about us only in terms of our sexual activity.

—DWIGHT STEVENS
New Relationships Paradigm Pioneer

Show the straight community the sides of us that are in loving relationships, that are compassionate human beings. Holding hands says a lot more about us being just the same as everyone else than groping each other on stage or in pride parades.

—J. JEFFREY HILL
Human Being

Discuss your homosexuality *as often as they discuss their heterosexuality*. Talk about your circle of friends, about how some are settling down in couples, some are going to a gay-singles ski weekend, some are being promoted at work, some are contemplating having children. Describe your new boyfriend or girlfriend. Tell them about the gay volleyball league you've joined or the lesbian bowling team. It's important for them to know that, just like straight people, you and other gay people of similar likes and dislikes get together in a variety of ways. It's important they understand that, contrary to the myths they might believe, your life is no more about sex than are the lives of most heterosexuals.

—MICHELANGELO SIGNORILE
Writer

Stop Worrying About What Others Think of You

Being openly gay in flamingly straight situations, you're forced to be more yourself. Your individuality comes to the fore, and you're able to bond with other people for reasons other than a shared sexual orientation, which isn't a bad thing. You start hanging out with people because you actually like them instead of because you're mutually oppressed.

—FRANK DECARO
Writer

There's no use in worrying about everyone else's feelings. . . . My life is my life, and they don't have a say in it.

—IAN ROBERTS
Professional Rugby Player

The picture is to ignore as much as you can the world's view of you and get on with your life and work.

—GORE VIDAL
Writer

Stop asking permission from the straight world to be who we are. It has nothing to do with them.

—BOY GEORGE
Singer

One of the things that I hate most of all is this notion that I have to serve as propaganda for straight people. I don't want to be a walking billboard showing straight people how good gay people can be or what our lives should be like. We have the right as individuals to live as we damn well please. I don't want to be anybody's billboard.

—DANIEL HARRIS
Writer

Dealing with Straights Who Give You Trouble

Sometimes people let the same problem make them miserable for years when they could just say, "So what." That's one of my favorite things to say. "So what. . . ." I don't know how I made it through all the years before I learned how to do that trick. It took a long time for me to learn it, but once you do, you never forget.

—ANDY WARHOL
Artist

What we've found is that if you let people know that you expect to be treated with dignity, that's how you'll be treated. That's not always the case, but it usually works. If you send the message that you expect to be treated like a second-class citizen, that you don't deserve to be treated well, then that's exactly how you'll be treated.

—ROD JACKSON
Model/Writer/Actor

Having a Positive Attitude Toward Homophobia

Homophobia is a disease, and we should try to develop compassion for the victims of this terrible affliction.

—BOB SMITH
Comic

Once you view homophobia as an affliction suffered by your parents and others, an affliction they have passed on to you, you begin to recognize that they don't know that their homophobia is destructive for you as well as for all gay people. You will find it easier to continue to love your family while at the same time understanding that they have a problem that endangers your emotional well-being.

—MICHELANGELO SIGNORILE
Writer

Retorts to Fag-Hating, Fundamentalist Christians

Judge not, that ye be not judged. — MATTHEW 7:1

If a man say, I love God, and hateth his brother, he is a liar: for he that loveth not his brother whom he hath seen, how can he love God whom he hath not seen?

—JOHN 4:20

If God hadn't made homosexuals, there wouldn't be any.

—1996 ATLANTA GAY PRIDE MARCH BANNER

Please know that Christ made you from His own image. If it's good enough for Him then why worry about mere mortals?

—E. LYNN HARRIS
Writer (from Just as I Am*)*

There were no tape recorders in those days and the guy they call jesus was wildly misquoted.

—DAVID WOJNAROWICZ
Writer/Performer

What do the leaders of that righteous institution of stone and stained glass say about a man who is over thirty, not married, lives with another man, kisses another man, and openly proclaims his love for another man? They call him a homosexual and, quoting from "that Book," condemn him straight to hell.

Well, Jesus was over thirty, not married, lived with twelve men, kissed Judas, and openly said He loved Peter. Think about it.

—E. THORNTON GOODE, JR.
Artist

If being gay is such a major sin, why isn't it in the Ten Commandments? If God hates gays more than any other sinners, why didn't He have His Son say a few words on the subject while He was here?

—SCOTT METZ
Writer/Illustrator

What to Say to People Who Think We Want Special Rights

It's you straights who have all the special rights. You straights have the special right to marry. You straights have the special right to be in the military, go out on a date with the person you love, talk about it the next day, and not get kicked out for it. You straights have the special right not to be prevented from visiting your loved one in the hospital. You straights have the special right to tax-free inheritance benefits. You straights have the special right to almost always have your loved ones covered under your work health-insurance policy. To say that gays and lesbians are asking for special rights is the height of lunacy.

—ELIJAH ELDERS
Angry Young Man

We are going to prevail just as every other component of the civil rights movement in this country has prevailed. There is nothing any of us can do today to stop that. We can embrace it warmly, as some of us do; we can resist it bitterly, as some of us do; but there is no power on earth that can stop it.

—GERRY STUDDS
Former U.S. Representative

What to Say to People Who Think We Shouldn't Have Children

Procreation is a force as old as the world itself, and we can barely begin to understand its deep and powerful rhythms. Homosexuals are not immune to its pull. I have a huge fatherhood impulse within me. To be a father, have kids, bring them up, teach and grow with them, would be an amazing thing.

—J. P. BETTS
Future Father and Vaguely Dissatisfied Faggot

Maybe fifty years from now there will be a tax credit for having a gay child.

—SIMON LEVAY
Scientist/Writer

Of course gay and lesbians should have children—but only those who fiercely want to. That's what makes queers such great moms and dads. Because we can't have our kids casually or by accident. If we want to have children, we have to overcome some basic biological and social obstacles. And a child who's wanted and cared about that strongly by his or her parents will be a very loved child. —JASON DARBY

Future Father

A lot of people are upset about gay parents. In South Carolina, a state representative wants to outlaw gay men and lesbians from adopting children because he believes gay households are "breeding grounds for future homosexuals."

I'm only going to explain this once: *Heterosexuals* are the breeding grounds for future homosexuals. I know it's hard to believe.

The idea that your parents influence your sexual orientation is ridiculous. Because if it were true, I'd have my mother's taste in men, and I've never dated a guy who falls asleep in his chair during *Jeopardy*! —BOB SMITH

Comic

I want kids, and I think that we as gay men ought to be able to have them. We often assume that it isn't an option. When my straight—and even some gay—friends find out about my goal of parenting, they ask how I plan on getting a kid. This is ridiculous. Straights get kids by and large by accident. We are creative. We can easily have our children, legally, by design. The real concern is: Can I care and provide for and love my child his/her whole life? That's the question gays and lesbians interested in children should ask, not: How do I get one?

—J. E. SALTERBERG
Uncle

What to Say to People Who Think We Shouldn't Be in the Military

We *are* this country's military. As someone who's been in the Navy for eleven years, I can say with complete certainty that the percentage of gays and lesbians in the military is significantly greater than in the general population.

—NAME WITHHELD BY REQUEST

An army should entirely consist of lovers and loved. . . . A handful of such men, fighting side by side, would defeat practically the whole world.

—PLATO

If they don't want us in the military, then I say that straight men can't be florists and straight women can't be UPS drivers.

—DANNY WILLIAMS
Comic

Nine to Five

The white, heterosexual male power structure that for the most part still controls American business has no motivation to let gays and lesbians into its ranks. Sure, they'll hire us and promote when we're valuable because of our skills. That's good business sense. But the lavender ceiling exists because the power structure will not willingly invite us into the upper echelons of power. Power is limited. Why would they share it? They need to hire us to make their companies strong and competitive; they don't need or want us to share in their power.

Solution? We must open our own businesses. Start our own franchises. Hire gay. Buy gay. We have to create our own power structure.

—JEFF HAYES
Small-Business Owner

Your sexuality and your career are two different things. Try to incorporate each into your whole life. Don't sacrifice one for the other. Don't choose a career because it's "gay," or easier to be gay in. You *can* have your cake and eat it, too.

—TOM KRECK
Physician

If you're like most slaves of capitalism, you work forty hours per week. This means that, most likely, you spend more of your conscious hours at work than in any other location. So come out, and if you're in a job where you feel you can't, then find a new job.

—PETE ACARE
Out at Work

Bring your partner to the company Christmas party, and let him dance with your boss.

—DUNCAN DAVIDSON
Architect

If someone at work has the balls to ask you if you're gay, tell them the truth.

—KEVIN RASMUSSEN
Gay Man and Life Partner

I'm a senior vice president at a five-hundred-plus-employee company. I keep a picture of my partner and me, arm in arm, on my desk at work. I know people talk, and I'm sure the existence of this photo is well known throughout the building. I want that so other gay and lesbian employees know that someone in upper-level management is openly gay and secure and successful within the company.

—ALLAN DELAINE
Executive

Don't Underestimate Your Family

Never underestimate your family; they can be a great source of support and love. We tell our families to accept us for who we are but then turn around and don't give them the opportunity to prove their love. I have been blessed with parents who surprise and teach me more and more what family is about. I think if more people opened their eyes and hearts, they could find the same support. —SCOTT SAMFORD
Marketing/Advertising—Account Services

Out of nowhere one day, my seventy-four-year-old grandmother asked for a picture of me and my boyfriend of five years. She said she'd been wanting a photo of us for years, and she'd been waiting for me to give her one. But I never did, so she figured she'd better ask. It had never occurred to me that she'd want a picture of us. I both misjudged and underestimated her. It was a huge lesson: Don't underestimate straights. Sometimes their homophobia is more my fear than their reality.

—RUSSELL GOLDSTEIN
Salesperson

About Parental Units

If we want our parents to accept us as gay, then we have to accept them as they are—even if they're gay-haters, as nonacceptable as they are. —RANDY OLSEN
Social Services

I compromised too much of myself in the past being a yes-man, trying to please everyone. At home, it was my role to keep the waters unruffled by being the peacemaker, the one to make concessions. My relationship with my mom has greatly improved since I came out to her. I've become more open, less guarded and tense with her; she can now know and appreciate me in all my colors.

Our comfort zones aren't the goal. Our love flows deeper than any differing viewpoints. We are neither one of us trying to be a people-pleaser. We're just matter-of-fact. The reactions are entirely up to the other person. We're not responsible for how the other person feels. My mom and I have a growing respect for our differences and a hope for the other's peace and happiness. I couldn't have achieved this hiding behind a wall as a pacifier. Pacifiers are for suckers.

—JOHN FARNSWORTH
Banker/Poet

Don't be surprised, when you come out to your family, if they're angry with you. If you grew up in a home where conflict and disagreement were covered up, then telling the truth will upset the family dynamic, regardless of what that truth is. It may take a couple of years for the members of your family to reach a new way of relating to one another. They cannot keep covering things up if you keep telling the truth about who you are and what your experiences are. Your coming out may change the way your entire family relates.

—RUSSELL DAVIS
Farm Boy

Take Back Your Power

Power is the object, not being tolerated. Fuck assimilation.

—TONY KUSHNER
Playwright (from Angels in America*)*

Stop trying to appeal to the mainstream so much. Labeling ourselves a minority gets us nowhere. The sympathy it buys from those few that are already receptive to us comes at an enormous price—and only ends with us further alienating ourselves by drawing attention to what makes us different.

—JOHN SOLBERG
Label-Free

We're constantly having conservative homosexuals say that we need to get married, to adopt children, join the army. . . . In effect the heterosexual is turned into a parent and we're saying we're nice children, and we're going to be just like you. I think it's very special to be homosexual and I don't want that kind of heterosexual shit put on me.

—JOHN RECHY
Writer

Your biological family cannot always be what you want them to be. Don't give them the power to hurt you if they don't like your sexuality. If they already have the power to hurt you, do what you must to *take that power back.*

—CHRISTOPHER COULTER
Still Growing

Don't Be a Victim

The Jews of Europe were victims. We must not be. We must never be grateful for mere crumbs off a table at which we have no place. Neither must we let ourselves be shamed from claiming our identity as gays, content instead to seek shelter under tents whose stakes are planted in the backs of our brothers and sisters.

—MARVIN LIEBMAN
Gay Activist

We refuse victim status, we constitute ourselves as history's agents rather than as its accidents, and even if that's only partly true, such a claim empowers us, and makes us grow too big for shackles, for kitchens, for closets, for ghettos of all kinds.

—TONY KUSHNER
Playwright

I'm not saying that in every instance and every place and every interaction a gay person has to be open about his emotional orientation in order to avoid victimhood; but I am saying that if he hides his orientation in a way no heterosexual would dream of doing, then he has actually acquiesced and contributed to the permanence of that victimhood.

—ANDREW SULLIVAN

Writer/Editor

Learn Self-Defense

Yes, it's getting better. Homophobia is lessening. But don't be lulled into false security: There are still plenty of people out there who *hate hate hate* you. Live your life with your eyes open.

—ROBERT BROWNE
Retail Slave

If we're being led away to concentration camps, I'm not going to go peacefully. Just the same, if people are going to bash us, we need to protect ourselves. That's not going to change the violent feelings people have in their hearts toward us, but it may make them think twice before picking up a baseball bat and trying to kill a gay man or lesbian.

—BOB PARIS
Bodybuilder/Activist/Writer

I was attacked and beaten up by a gang of teenagers one October night on my walk home from work. There were five or six of them, and I didn't fight back, as two had a hold of each of my arms. Instinct told me to be passive, to not resist. I numbed out and listened to my inner voice, which crooned an "everything will be okay" lullaby as their fists and feet pummeled me. When they stuck the gun in my face, I honestly laughed inside. I was thinking, "Yeah—as if I'm not already scared?"

My ensuing anger over the next few months taught me never again to allow myself to be in such a vulnerable position. I am more muscular now, and sometimes I intimidate people. It makes me laugh to think that *they* watch their step around *me* now. Self-protection can be a distancing, double-edged sword, yet I prefer it to feeling helpless. No one else is going to take care of me but me. Even though there may be consequences, it is okay to stand up for myself. And I am certain that if there ever is a next time, I will go down swinging.

—JOHN FARNSWORTH
Banker/Poet

If you are attacked by a basher, do *not* think of your assailant as a human being. He is an animal, and you must do whatever is necessary to protect yourself.

—TAYLOR DANES
Self-Defense Instructor

Living Well *Is* the Best Revenge

Every morning I wake up with a smile on my face, every friend I hold and comfort through his pain, every gay book I read, every time I walk down the street holding my boyfriend's hand, I am winning the war. I am telling Jesse Helms and his kindred to fuck off. I am saying: Yes, you hate me. You've tried to do everything you could to hurt me. But I am still alive. I'm surviving. I am happy.

I say: Live well. It's our revenge.

—THOMAS SHAW
Pharmacist

"It's a Queer World, After All"

Don't Let Others Define You

Beware of men who say things like "This is what gay is; now be that way if you're gay." They're as fanatic as the religious right.

—CHRISTOPHER ELMER
Friend to Myself

To be categorized is, simply, to be enslaved. Watch out.

—GORE VIDAL
Writer

Too many people are hung up about whether it's heterosexuality, homosexuality, whatever sexuality. . . . People should get over it and get on with their lives.

—IAN ROBERTS
Professional Rugby Player

"Homosexual" and "heterosexual" describe *acts*, not people. Think of the word "gay" as meaning happiness in sexual freedom and the elimination of outdated, strict paradigms, not an eternal assignment to homosexual sex. —TIMOTHY GRANT

Computer Systems Manager

Men were falling in love with each other long before they began calling themselves gay. By declining to ask or answer the question of who I am, I can, with courage, allow myself many selves and multiple possibilities. . . . If I tell you, "I'm a gay man," I am making an exclusionary statement. More than anything else, I am telling you *what* I am not: I am not a man who has sex with women. But I'm revealing very little of who—a Southerner, a political writer who shuttles back and forth between the power obsessions of Washington and the pixilated marginality of San Francisco, a would-be actor who grows apples in Kentucky and is learning to make champagne cider—I am. —FRANK BROWNING

Writer

Labeling is so self-limiting. We are what we do—not what we say we are.

—MONTGOMERY CLIFT
Actor

The Gay label doesn't really bother me, as long as it's just not something that is restrictive. I just don't think one should live one's life as a Gay man. I don't think that sexuality necessarily implies a life-style package that comes with it.

—NEIL TENNANT
(of the Pet Shop Boys) Singer/Songwriter

Defining yourself as gay is just like defining yourself as an American, or a Jew, or whatever. You may play within a subgroup, but you'll never feel fulfillment as long as you define yourself that way. Your fulfillment in the universe is on many, many levels.

—RAM DASS
Spiritual Activist/Author

I have no idea what it means to be gay. Most of my friends are gay (though lesbians are usually more interesting), I hang out in gay bars, and I regularly flirt with other men. I've even taught gay literary theory. And yet, at some point—I don't know when—"gay" no longer mattered as much, and I started worrying about just getting through, hopefully in the company of like-minded people (some of whom I might have sex with occasionally).

—DAVID SCHULZ
Writer

I hear so much quibbling and grumbling about what we should call ourselves. Guys my age (in their forties) seem to get their feathers ruffled when teens refuse to call themselves gay because "gay" is so limiting. And guys in their fifties and older bust their gasket about others calling themselves fairies or queer, because for so long those were pejorative labels.

But I say, So what? Let every man call himself what he wants. The freedom to choose our identity, choose our label—if any at all—is really what everyone was fighting for, wasn't it?

—EDDIE LEIGH
Businessman

Be Whoever, Whatever, and However You'd Like

If you're going to be gay, you might as well be fabulous. It's a birthright.

—FRANK DECARO
Writer

When you break the norm, that's when you have a chance to sparkle. The people who get in trouble, who say "Fuck you" to the normal processes, are the ones who float or die.

—TODD OLDHAM
Fashion Designer

I hope that style has no limits; for me, style is a human being who says, "I will wear a feather to the funeral. I will dare to be happy.

—PAUL RUDNICK
Writer

Who says men can't wear this particular item of clothing? Or this color? Or makeup? Why not?

—JAMES M. SASLOW
Historian/Writer

There was one friend—"Prissy" was his name—who was a real role model for me because he knew how to do everything. He could sew, he could make dresses, he knew how to do drag, he knew how to make a delicious meal with four dollars, and he could fix his truck. And I thought, That's it! That's the way to be. No limits at all.

—WILL ROSCOE
Writer/Anthropologist

I was watching *Pillow Talk* on TV, and in that movie Tony Randall seems gay, and Rock Hudson seems straight—and it's the reverse. It's good to break down those stereotypes, because obviously gay people come in all styles and fashions.

—CHRISTOPHER DURANG
Playwright

Style

One should either be a work of art, or wear a work of art. —OSCAR WILDE
Writer

Gay style is too expansive to be called "gay style." I think it's more important to understand where it's coming from. Are we being manipulated by consumerism, or are we directing it? Don't follow the style of others. Re-create it to fit your personality and mood. I wear pearl earrings with a black leather jacket. And, boy, do I feel swell.

—LARRY ALDRICH
Happy-Go-Lucky Pedestrian

Stop following trends. The word *trend* will no longer have any meaning as we all dress and behave only in the exact manner we choose, proving ourselves as true individuals.

—TODD OLDHAM
Designer

I get tired of the arcane need to be in a mold, to be a clone. Maybe before Stonewall there was a need; it was a dangerous time to be gay. One could more easily be arrested or blackmailed, or lose one's job. There was more of a need for a secret society or look. Now let's diversify.

—MARK FLEMING
Sacred Intimate and Healer

I get tired of hearing the pissing and moaning about clones. Because people who choose to wear clone costumes are choosing to be publicly homosexual. I think that's a political act itself. I would endorse them over any coat-and-tie faggot any day of the week.

—ARMISTEAD MAUPIN
Writer

Flamboyance

If you want to be a nelly queen, be one out of joy, not desperation. I hate to watch someone drowning in his own flamboyance.

—SCOTT PERRET
Writer/Actor/Director

Those who dress provocatively and trashy are just insecure and need to be noticed. However, if it's the only thing one can do, then by all means do it, and hopefully get over it.

—MR. BLACKWELL
Designer and Fashion Cop

Shake up the general populace and make them think. Wear glitter. Be camp. Do drag. Let out your faerie spirit. It's part of being gay, healing through challenging.

—MARK FLEMING
Sacred Intimate and Healer

Camp It Up

Camp may be gay culture's most effective weapon and most unique contribution to the culture wars. Camp infiltrates the enemy with its own devices and subverts strategies of containment. Camp turns weapons of oppression inside out; camp explodes while it entertains.

—DAVID SCHULZ
Writer

Let's start paying attention to what we're doing with this humor, this teasing camp humor, that brings everyone down to the same level. It creates a social contract and a social space and points out where your ego is inflated, or where your self-image is out of whack with your looks. . . . It establishes equality among participants.

—WILL ROSCOE
Writer/Anthropologist

Drag

Don't you dare knock drag unless you've tried it.

—BRENT PONTON
Actor

If you're going to do drag, dress as a woman to honor femininity, not to mock or scorn it.

—RAND MASTERS
Sometime Drag Queen

Drag should be the ultimate. And if you can afford to do the ultimate, then do the ultimate. I mean, drag should always be the best you can afford it to be.

—HARVEY FIERSTEIN
Playwright/Actor

If you've never gone in drag, if you've never hung out with some gay guys while they're in drag in public, I don't think that you've made the progress toward self-acceptance that you need to make. You've got to learn to feel comfortable with the most outrageous and sometimes degraded images of us. —WILL ROSCOE

Writer/Anthropologist

If you're a straight man, you should do it at least once in your life. If you're a gay man, at least once a month.

—ALEXIS ARQUETTE

Actor

Being involved in cross-dressing is a way of laying claim to all the possible archetypes of the universe. It's all about symbols, right? Gay men do not generally dress up as housewives from Peoria. If you're going to do this, you tend to dress up as somebody larger than life. If you're going to live outside of normal social rules and regulations, you might as well upgrade. Aim high! —JAMES M. SASLOW

Historian/Writer

Get Over Beauty

Beauty is a complete waste of time: because without even knowing it, we still cringe in the shadow of classical ideals of beauty. The Greeks were mad about the human body—so much so, that during its heyday, Athens must have looked like an outfitter's window during a weavers' strike. But it was no help—not one of the great classical statues has the least physical individuality which would make it desirable or even interesting. So beauty you will never need.

—QUENTIN CRISP
Writer/Actor

I ain't sayin' I never fell for a pretty face, but when *les jeux sont faits* . . . give me a toad with a pot of gold and I'll give ya three meals a day. 'Cause honeys, ain't no such thing as a toad when the lights go down. It's either feast or famine. It's the daylight you gotta watch out for. Face it, a thing of beauty is a joy till sunrise.

—HARVEY FIERSTEIN
Playwright (from Torch Song Trilogy*)*

Never get mad because there are better-looking guys than you. The potential for better-looking is infinite.

—ETHAN MORDDEN

Writer (from How Long Has This Been Going On?*)*

And heaven's grace as well
Reminds me to accept what hurts the eyes,
For, looked at often, ugliness soon dies.

—MICHELANGELO

Painter/Sculptor/Writer/General Connoisseur of Human Beauty

I'm an overweight, nonmuscular aging man who couldn't be prouder of who he is. I have no problem with it. If anyone else does, it's really their problem, and I sincerely suggest that they deal with it.

—DAVID MIXNER

Activist

I was in the market, wearing some shorts and a tight T-shirt. Some ditsoid queen walked by and said under his breath, but intentionally loud enough for me to hear, "Look at her. She shouldn't be allowed in public wearing that frock." I say: Fuck you. I am so sick of people telling me that I can't wear a tight T-shirt or short shorts because my body isn't good enough. I have a body, and I am perfectly satisfied with it, even though it's not lean or muscular. Who says that you can show your body only if it mirrors the gym bodies? Should people who don't have model-quality faces put bags over their heads? Should men with whiny voices never open their mouths? I am going to wear what I want, and show whatever parts of my body I want, even if I am fifty pounds overweight. If the sight of my bulging stomach offends you, then put blinders over your eyes.

—GRADY DELMORE
Couch Potato

Don't feel you need to voice your opinion about how cute or not cute every guy you meet is.

—REYNOLD EVERETT
Handyman

Be an iconoclast. Dare to be gay and *not* have muscles.

—JEFFREY HOLT
143-Pound Weakling

Get Beyond Surfaces

A person has many layers. In the late twentieth century, we tend to focus on the retail layer.

We have been trained to look at, look for, certain appearances. We test each person's ability to mimic the images advertisers create to inspire longing in us all. We toss aside so many hearts this way. Another J. Crew casualty.

It has not stopped at the clothes. Advertisers sell mood, feeling, longing, image, so that our very faces and bodies have become subject to retail analysis. Impatiently, then, we thrash through the piles of people we see, looking for the one that will at once enflame and quell our desires as deftly and exactly as that haunting Calvin Klein underwear print ad.

And when we look in the mirror at night, we weep or grow proud, depending on what we see.

Advice?

We owe it to one another to graduate from gay high school. Seeing one another in the bars, on the streets, at the gym, let us strive to make respect the first instinct, and let the assessment of beauty and potential be more private and, ultimately, more generous. Let our eyes seek out the humanity first, and the crotch or the pectoral muscle more discreetly.

—SCOTT PERRET
Writer/Actor/Director

So many of us seem overly attached to things—having the right label on the inside of our sweater, owning hand towels that perfectly match the shower curtain, or being the first to buy, own, and show off whatever Madison Avenue is effectively pushing. It's as though if we have the correct accoutrements, then somehow we're more desirable or worth more. It's a trap that all of America seems to fall into, but sometimes I think gay men are more susceptible. I hate to see other gay men let their lives be ruled by their possessions. It's time for us to break free. De-materialize.

—AARON MICHAELS
Proud Slacker

The Ghetto

I grew up in a small town in Pennsylvania. Moving to a large city and living in a gay ghetto changed my life. I discovered I was not alone. There's a big world out there. Go live where you feel comfortable. Life is too damn short to stay where you don't like.

—JOHN J. GANCAR II
Educator

No matter what, don't try to fit into the gay world and its ideas just because you don't fit into the so-called straight world. Have your own world.

—JASON DRIVER

Lots of us leave the hetero world because we don't fit in so well. Then we come into the gay world and allow others to define who we are here. Don't conform; be yourself. There are many, many flavors of gay life.

—MARK C. MICHAEL
Clinical Psychologist and Alpine Hiking Guide

Every now and then, take a vacation where you're away from homos. It's good to spend a little time out of the comfort zone and learn to enjoy it.

—STEPHAN ARNETT
Travel Agent

Live with a lesbian so you learn that penises don't rule.

—SCOTT OLSEN
Male-Gender Lesbian

When you come out, keep your straight friends. The ghetto mentality gets boring after a while.

—ALLAN HOLLINGSWORTH
Writer

If you spend too long in all-gay scenarios—gay bars, gay restaurants, gay Lycra dealerships—the temptation to adopt a ghetto mentality becomes irresistible. You stop being yourself and start being just another short-haired guy with a weakness for Grace Jones albums. Gayness threatens to become your raison d'être at the expense of all the other parts of your character. We're all well-rounded creatures, or at least we should try to be.

—FRANK DECARO
Writer

Pride

Why does "Gay Pride" mean liberating old Bob Mackie gowns and creating a dead-movie-star parade? What do we hope to gain with these actions—the right to suck cock during the national anthem?

The best part of dignity, self-respect, and worth, "pride" is not a verb. It resides strong and still. Being gay just is. The need to prove it deletes the point. It just is.

—FRANK RATTÉ
Human Being

A new generation, born of the Stonewall explosion, would choose to think of itself as positively *gay*—except for one nagging doubt: gay pride! No matter how noble the sentiment, no matter how passionate the intent, slogans like "Two, four, six, eight, gay is just as good as straight!" end up implying that being gay is *almost* as good as straight.

—HARRY HAY
Queer Activist and Founding Father of Radical Faeries

Black Pride and Gay Pride are dangerous slogans like White Pride or Straight Pride. Gay and Black are not achievements but accidents of birth. One must not be ashamed, but that's not the same as being proud. Pride should lie only in what one does with one's Blackness or Gayness.

—NED ROREM
Writer

I've heard people say it's ridiculous to be proud of one's gayness, because that's like being proud of your blond curls or your long eyelashes. To be proud of something, you have to accomplish something.

Those people miss the point. I'm not proud of *being* gay; I'm proud of publicly announcing it to the world. I grew up in a painfully repressed and repressive family. I've never once, not to this day, seen my father in a short-sleeved shirt or with his top collar button undone. I never went out in public with an open collar until I was twenty-two. I didn't know what masturbation was until my college roommate explained it to me. I lost my virginity, with a woman, at age twenty-eight, probably not a world record, but damn close to it, I imagine. I didn't have my first experience with a man until I was thirty-five, and I didn't come out until I was forty-one. I loathed myself for being attracted to men. I thought I was dirty and sick. But I've grown. I've accepted myself, and I like being gay now.

When I look back over the journey I've made, from a complete basket case to a place of relative mental health, from a place of fiery self-hatred to a place of satisfied acceptance, I am very, very proud of myself. I'm sure some people's journeys are much more dramatic than mine, and others are less dramatic. But in this world as it is, where homophobia still abounds, being able to stand up straight and verbalize "I am gay and I like it" is an act that's completely worthy of pride.

—C. J. MORRITZ
Proud Gay Man

Create the Family You Want

The world looks at the family unit in such an extraordinarily limited way. I can live alone, and I am a family. I can live with my partner (or not live with him), and we are a family. I can live with close, cherished friends (or not live with them), and we are a family. I can have children or not, and we'd be a family. My family is whatever and however I define it. It seems to me the height of insanity to let the IRS or my medical plan or some archaic laws tell me who my family is.

—EDWARD L. ARNETT
Banker

You *can* choose your family. Sometimes they may be biological, sometimes not. Who you allow into your life as your family is your choice.

—SAM WHITING
Actor Cum Activist

Queer Spirituality

Next time you're stumbling down the street, having dragged yourself out of bed at noon for your Sunday fag brunch, and you see that homo in his coat and tie exiting church, keep your puzzled or nasty looks to yourself. There *are* gay Christians, so stop getting freaked out by that, because it's not going to change.

—BRENT PONTON
Actor

Do not underestimate the power of your spirit. Do not believe that your life, your being, is less than tremendous. You are already bigger than the Smith Tower. Pity is out of the question; I will love you instead. And if you eventually give in and love yourself, well, then there is no stopping you.

So take one tiny step today. Pick up the Tao Te Ching or Deepak Chopra or, if you can bear it, the Bible, or a good novel or a self-help book. Go to an art gallery or a movie or sit in your room and be still. And then pursue the part that rings true, the part that makes your heart ache with beauty, joy, or sadness, the part that makes your heart still. Look at it. Let it be. And let yourself be, in the face of it. Notice it. Notice you.

There. You're already alive.

This is one moment. It is all there is, and it is only one in countless thousands. The world is a rich place. You are in it. Weep. Rejoice. —SCOTT PERRET

Writer/Actor/Director

Don't let anyone tell you that gay men and lesbians are not spiritual. Or that to come out means to reject religion or God. Was the church you were raised in toxic toward gays? Leave it behind and find a new one. If the name Jesus or Jehovah makes you flinch, then you have some healing to do. —RUSSELL DAVIS

Farm Boy

Don't believe men who say that if you love God, you have to deny your own nature.

—CHRISTOPHER ELMER
Friend to Myself

Spirituality is the most important element of my existence. Strive for the spiritual that is ecumenical, universal, and positive. Its *name* is irrelevant, and it has no established following, because it has survived and will survive humanity—the very humanity that has often condemned our existence and spirituality. Try not to be blinded by the rhetoric of the religious, but listen and embrace the spirituality that speaks to your inner being. The inner core that connects and electrifies all life is the source of peace and harmony. Go to the source; it's within you and all life.

—ROBERT L. GIRON
Poet/Writer/Educator

“*Love, Sex, and the Whole Damn Thing*”

Be a Lover

Love him and let him love you. Do you think anything else under heaven really matters?

—JAMES BALDWIN
Writer

Be not shy of the love you can share with other men. Fear of love is fear of the sublime. Put lovemaking before moneymaking and troublemaking. To be a lover is to practice the major art of life. You must love even if it hurts. It will hurt more if you don't love.

—JAMES BROUGHTON
Writer/Filmmaker/Poet

Love is no use unless it's wise, and kind, and undramatic. Something steady and sweet, to smooth out your nerves when you're tired. Something tremendously cosy; and unflurried by scenes and jealousies.

—NOEL COWARD
Playwright (from Private Lives*)*

You can't apologize for falling in love. You *shouldn't* apologize for falling in love. Falling in love . . . is a victory.

—ROBERT RODI
Writer (from Kept Boy*)*

All the wonderful things you've heard about love are true. Love finds a way, love changes your outlook, love joins you not only with another human being, but with the best in yourself. Never underestimate the power of love, or yourself as lover. Love is the sweet word that heals: It can save you. Be a lover. Lovers are always winners. Love.

—DAVID LOOVIS
Writer

Down on Love

Love, love, love. I'm so sick of hearing about love. Get a dog, get a cat, get a parrot and teach it to say "I love you" if that's what you're so desperate to hear. I've been single and celibate now for seven years, and I may be a bitchy queen at times, but I know I'm the better for it.

—ALEX RUMINES
Landscaper

I don't like the word love. It's like patriotism. It's like the flag. It's the last refuge of scoundrels. When people start talking about what wonderful, warm, deep emotions they have and how they love people, I watch out. Somebody is going to steal something.

—GORE VIDAL
Writer

Responsible Love

A gay guy comes into the restaurant, and I know I can probably double the amount of the tip I'll get by turning on the charm, doing the flirt thing. But I try hard not to do that. You've got to be responsible with your flirting, because it can be a mind-fuck. Of course, once [a famous, rumored-to-be-gay actor] came in, and I flirted my ass off. And I walked home with a hundred-dollar bill!

—BOBBY JARVIS
Waiter

Learn your body's language. By this I mean that you are always sending signals to others with your body. There are so many guys who are oblivious to the signals they send through their body language, and it's not fair to the rest of us. If you learn what your posture conveys, what the way you hold your hands suggests, and so on, then you cannot send misleading signals.

—TERRY BERTRUM
Yoga Instructor

Don't Lie About Your HIV Status

You don't have to tell some guy you're HIV-positive. I mean, if a guy I'm dating asks me, I'm not going to lie. But I'm not going to volunteer the info, either. I mean, if he needs to know so bad, then he can ask me.

—CRAIG POPSIL
Sales Manager

I am so tired of liars. You know, you're two weeks or two months into the relationship, and he says real casually, "Oh, by the way, I'm HIV-positive." All I ask, just tell me up front, okay? Don't wait.

—STEVE AMES
Office Manager

Stop Searching for Prince Charming

Someday your prince will come. Only it may not be with you. So get over the myth of Prince Charming. It's a very destructive myth.

—GRAY HOBSON
Retired Engineer

Learn from the English tabloids: Princes (with or without shining armor) do not make good husbands.

—ZACH LARSON
No Longer Looking for a Prince

Stop looking for Mr. Right and set about *becoming* Mr. Right.

—GREGORY FLOOD
Writer

Forget Jeff Stryker

If you are forty pounds overweight, rather than accept the standard of gay male god-worship, why don't you try to eroticize yourself and go after people who look like you? . . . If you're bald, rather than chase Jeff Stryker around the dance floor, look for someone like me who thinks it's way hot.

—MICHAEL CALLEN
Activist/Author

Beware of men who look like Adonis but couldn't tell you who he was.

—SAM WHITING
Actor Cum Activist

I'm guilty of it myself, but youth and beauty worship is *stupid*! And self-defeating. So many of my friends want to date/fuck only really young guys. If they keep this attitude, they will never have a long-term relationship and be happy.

—PATRICK BROWNE
Doctor and Film Critic

Get over your sexual "type." That's been the most liberating accomplishment of my life. How? I allowed myself to be with some well-intended, knowledgeable, and horny men who weren't in my type spectrum. And I discovered that even though they weren't my type, their love was valid, nourishing, and desirable.

—MALCOLM McKAY
Erotic Activist

Talk About Sex

It's important for us to talk about sex, to define ourselves in a world which has never talked about us or even let us talk about ourselves. If people can't understand that, they are very foolish. When you start to talk, it confirms you are living.

—DEREK JARMAN
Film Director

When life no longer presents the occasion for sex it should present the near occasion; that is, we should talk about it endlessly . . . talk with open minds, realizing that talking about sex is dangerous because talking about sex makes us want to do it.

—TONY KUSHNER
Playwright

Be Inventive in Bed

If you want your lover to treat you as a woman while you're in bed, fine, go ahead and do it. If you want him to string you up or chain you down or if you want to have sex while eating bananas, whatever, do it. There's a kind of divine irresponsibility in the bedroom, and that sense of following your fantasies, of generating them, nourishing them, and exploring them is all very useful.

— EDMUND WHITE
Writer

Don't be afraid to be inventive in bed, but if somebody asks you to do "the Piñata," send them your regrets.

—ROMAN HANS
Writer

Know that an erection is not essential (and in fact can be counterproductive) to fabulous lovemaking.

—DWIGHT STEVENS
Erotic Progressive

The three components of great sex are volume, originality, and enthusiasm. One without the other two is a recipe for, at best, mediocrity. Two out of three ain't bad. But all three—*that's* a sex life that will endure.

—ELI HERBERT

Salesclerk

Take Responsibility for HIV

If a group of people can dress Nancy Reagan so she looks moderately attractive, they certainly can find ways to make safe sex interesting. —VITO RUSSO

Writer/Film Historian/Critic

I hear and read of some HIV-positive gay men who believe it's the responsibility of the HIV-negative gay men to protect themselves, that if a guy is willing to have unsafe sex, it means he's already positive, so it's okay. Well, that's not always true. There are many HIV-negative gay men having unsafe sex, for reasons it would take a full book to explain. And just because some HIV-negative man has low enough self-esteem, or is ignorant about safe sex, or doesn't care if he gets it or not, whatever the reason, I do not want to be the one who infects him. I believe that an HIV-positive gay man has a responsibility as a human being not to spread the virus, regardless if the other person cares or not.

—GARY FRANKLIN
Regular Guy

The government is not giving us HIV.
The Christian Right is not giving us HIV.
We are giving HIV to each other.
It's up to us to save our tribe.

—JOHN LEONARD
Seattle AIDS Educator and Community Activist

Try using an anal condom. They're meant for women, but they give the receptive partner in whatever type of sex more control—you can put it in and not rely on or ask the other person to wear a rubber on his dick. Also, there's less constriction, so guys who hate to wear traditional rubbers may not be so unhappy with the anal ones.

—SANDY McCULLEM
Sex Educator

Set Your Boundaries

Remember, you are always in control of your cock and what comes out of it, as well as your butt and what goes into it, not to mention all the other chunks of your body you might choose to use during some nocturnal play. It is always up to you to set and stick to your boundaries.

—ANDREW ANSEN
Businessman

When having sex, there is *never* a point of no return. If he does something you don't like, ask him to stop. *Tell* him to stop.

—CHRISTOPHER COULTER
Still Growing

When I was first coming out, there were plenty of times I felt obligated to give sex to people that I didn't really want to. I thought that since dinner was paid for and he showed interest, that meant there was some contractual obligation. A younger cousin of mine came out to me, right before his sixteenth birthday. I warned him about this, what I learned: You don't ever have to do things sexually that you don't want to do.

—NAME WITHHELD

Stranger, unless with bedroom eyes
I beckon you to fraternize,
Beware of rudely crossing it:
I have no gun, but I can spit.

—W. H. AUDEN
Poet

Be a Dick Hound

Be a dick hound if that's what you want. I'm a dick hound. I mean, straights always criticize us. You know, all we think about is dick, dick, dick. But you think straight guys aren't always thinking about pussy? We're just more honest about it.

—JOSH HARRIS
Plumber

If you want to fuck around, that's fine; I'm not going to be an old auntie and say, "Don't fuck around." But if you're going to make fucking around your be-all and end-all, don't complain that you haven't found the lover you want.

—LARRY KRAMER
Writer/Activist

We need to be indiscriminate. No one should be denied love because they are old, ugly, fat, crippled, bruised, of the wrong race, color, creed, sex or country of national origin. We need to copulate with anyone who requests our company.

—CHARLES SHIVELY
Writer

Get yourself fucked if you want to. Get yourself anything you like. Reject all the values of the society. And enjoy sex. When you're dead, you'll regret not having fun with your genital organs.

—JOE ORTON
Playwright

In a mad way, perhaps one-night stands are potentially more spiritual, more demanding, more extraordinary than anything else!

—CHRISTOPHER ISHERWOOD
Writer

Don't treat your trick like a trick.

—SLUGGER
Retired Party Boy

I don't think there's anything wrong with relating to people on the level of pure meat, as long as you don't get trapped into that all the time as a single level of consciousness—as some queens do.

—ALLEN GINSBERG
Poet

Be Careful with Anonymous Sex

Anonymous sex is like alcohol. Some people can dabble and be okay. Others will spiral out of control. Understand your reasons for participating in anonymous sex. Know that most likely, the reasons for wanting anonymous sex are deeper than a mere sexual need for release. Past abuse and/or low self-esteem are pretty common denominators to being out of control with sex. Seek to resolve these past issues.

—DARRIN MORGAN
AIDS Service Organization Employee

The Endless Monogamy Debate

How any two people handle this issue is a matter of personal choice and shouldn't be subject to anyone's approval. Unfortunately, people try to pass judgment on the legitimacy of gay relationships based on whether or not a couple is monogamous. If we applied that test to heterosexual marriages, the majority of those relationships would have to be considered invalid. So if you're going to hold gay couples up to that standard, then you better damn well hold up the entire world to it. Monogamy or nonmonogamy has no bearing on the legitimacy or the quality of a relationship, as long as both partners agree to whatever arrangement they have. —ROD JACKSON

Actor/Writer/Model

Some men want a sexually monogamous relationship. Others want an open one. I say, whatever works. But independent of sexual behavior, I think emotional monogamy is essential for maintaining a successful relationship. I can deal with my boyfriend's dick being with some other guy. I don't think I could deal with his heart being there, too.

—BRAD JASPERS
Husband of Twelve Years

Couples should celebrate having a successful relationship. Like my boyfriend and me: After we've been faithful a year, we get one night of fun.

—ROMAN HANS
Writer

I can't tell with these "Make 'em up as you go along" rules. Monogamy's a much easier system to keep track of.

—HARVEY FIERSTEIN
Playwright (from Torch Song Trilogy*)*

Be creative in defining your lover relationship. We aren't exactly following the hetero model, so why not accept some real differences in how we define our primary relationship? Go with what seems to work for you, regardless of how it compares to the traditional, hetero approach. Maybe you and your partner will live apart or appear more to be very close friends than lovers. As long as you both agree to your style, forget about that traditional model of romance. —MARK C. MICHAEL

Clinical Psychologist and Alpine Hiking Guide

I had a successful open relationship for seven years. We agreed up front on our rules: We had sex outside the relationship only somewhere other than our home. We agreed to immediately stop seeing the other man if it started to become emotional and not just sexual. We planned quality time together. We agreed ahead of time on a specific night when we would both go looking for sex with someone other than each other. We made specific times to reevaluate what was and wasn't working. It took a great deal of respect and communication—but it worked. —DWIGHT STEVENS

New Relationships Paradigm Pioneer

Relearn Sex as Sacred

Relearn sex as sacred, playful, nonaddictive, noncompulsive, and nonstop.

—JOSEPH KRAMER
Sexual Healer

Novalis said, "There is only one temple in the world, and that is the human body." . . . The proper activity in a temple is worship. Open your temple to love. Visit other temples. . . . Believe in the unbelievable, worship wonder, and celebrate life.

—JAMES BROUGHTON
Writer/Filmmaker/Poet

Touch your anus, lick hidden places, and risk God.

—MATT SILVERSTEIN
Sex Activist

Humankind is struggling with understanding what sexuality is all about. And gays are a very predominant sexual specialty in terms of the power they carry. . . . To gay men I say: Just stop whatever you're doing and go inside. Find your inner Guide and wake up. There's nothing more awesome than sexual union with God.

—ED STEINBRECHER
Author

Integrate Sex and Emotion

It seems to me that the real clue to your sex-orientation lies in your romantic feelings rather than in your sexual feelings. If you are really gay, you are able to fall in love with a man, not just enjoy having sex with him.

—CHRISTOPHER ISHERWOOD
Writer

Have pride as a bottom. Reject society's unspoken insinuation that somehow you're less of a man if you're a bottom.

—DUANE TAYLOR
Out Bottom

The men you want to sleep with so you'll feel beautiful, or validated, or to calm your angers and fears and insecurities—leave those men alone. Sleep only with the men you honestly want to share something with.

—ROBERT HOLZMEIER
Queer Activist

Throughout childhood, I was often shamed and ridiculed for being too emotional, too like a girl. I learned early on that letting someone else see who I really was usually led to trouble. When I became sexually active, that pattern continued: I rarely expressed emotion during sex. I became such an amazing sexual performer—I'd mow the guy over, he'd be too exhausted to think about my needs. I'd never give a guy a chance to truly see me or touch me. I was such a great sex machine because I was terrified of being seen as human. This led to major resentments on my part, which eventually led to self-searching. I began to understand the huge separation between my heart and my cock. In childhood, if I wasn't seen, I was safe. In adulthood, that formula didn't work. Now the secret to great sex is being seen for who I am.

—MARK FLEMING
Sacred Intimate and Healer

Your sexuality is no different from your money supply in that you must use it wisely if you expect it to produce good results for you. Use it poorly and, with sex as with money, you will have nothing to show for it finally but bills to be paid.

—GREGORY FLOOD

Writer

Oy, the Terminology

I disagree with the term "alternative family." My life partner and I have been together for thirteen years, and we have jointly adopted three children. We teach our kids that all family is chosen. Husbands and wives choose one another, as well as same-sex people. And all choose whether or not to have children. We call ourselves a family, period.

—MICHAEL SERKIN-POOLE
Full-time Dad

It's awfully difficult to know what to call the one you're seeing these days. When I came out, you either had a trick or lover. Simple as that! But, today, there are as many different labels for the person you're seeing or going out with as there are different kinds of breakfast cereals. Recently a friend said to me, "Although George and I are in love with one another, we are partners in life." Well, lighten up! Sounds to me as though they've formed a law firm. Doesn't "significant other" make you just want to puke? Just picture this yuppie publicist sitting in his swanky Beverly Hills office trying to come up with a new buzz phrase for Dr. Joyce Brothers to introduce on *The Tonight Show.* "Significant Other." Much too clinical to me. Then there's "mate," if you happen to be sea-worthy! Or "life mate," if you're interested in a prison sentence. And there's always the good old standbys of "spouse" and "other half," but they smack too much of the heterosexual world and tend to be demeaning. Trick and lover still say it all to me.

—R. G. TALBERT
Writer/Actor

Really Talk to Him

I've been living with my boyfriend for almost five years and fucking around behind his back for three and a half. And it's never safe fucking around, it's always down and dirty, wet and nasty, everything-you're-not-supposed-to-do sex. The safe sex only happens with my boyfriend.

I've never tested positive—*thank God*—for anything in my life, except maybe my attitude, so I've been lucky so far. But I really want to stop risking my life. And his. I really do love him.

I have tried to get help: I saw a shrink for a while—an older guy who liked getting his dick sucked while he squatted over me on his couch. I went to a counselor, too, in the social services building—and got fucked in the garage storage room by the parking attendant. I even went to a few Sex Addicts Anonymous meetings—I stopped going back after I realized how much the group's leader liked me to watch him take a piss during break. But even with all this, I couldn't get my sex life under control.

Recently, however, I went to my doctor for my annual HIV test and lecture. But instead of his usual Russian roulette speech, he asked me what I was *feeling* when I was out in search of stranger cock.

I thought about it—that hungry feeling of emptiness that needs to be filled by something *big*. The loneliness. The insecurity. The sadness. I told the doctor that I want to feel loved, to feel handsome, to feel desired and wanted.

My doctor suggested I give my boyfriend the opportunity to fulfill my needs, that I tell my boyfriend when I feel lonely, or scared, or ugly, or worthless. He said that maybe my boyfriend could give me some of the things I hoped to find with strangers. I agreed to give it a try.

I talked to my boyfriend. I told him when I felt lonely. And frustrated. And ugly and stupid and unlovable. And you know what? I kept talking. And talking and talking and talking. And now we've been talking—*I mean really talking*—for three months.

And it's been three months since I've fucked around. Really.

—SERGIO ST. TROPEZ
(Unemployed) Dance Instructor

Talk About the Negative Stuff

I see relationships falling apart all the time. Perhaps the most destructive trait I see is the men's inability to express their anger and hurt and other so-called negative feelings with each other. You don't want to hurt your partner. You don't want to cause waves. Yet not expressing the negative emotions will hurt more and cause bigger and more hurtful waves down the line.

If there's one piece of advice I could offer, it's this: Commit to talking about the negative feelings, no matter how difficult they are.

—VINCE LEE
Therapist

You can't be afraid to argue. . . . If you really love each other, you'll be able to survive the arguments.

—BOB PARIS
Bodybuilder/Activist/Writer

Don't Ever Hit Him

You don't—you can't, you shouldn't—beat up somebody you love (no matter what fantasies are being fed).

—MARTIN DUBERMAN
Historian/Writer

Hitting someone you're in a relationship with is never okay unless it's in self-defense, and if your relationship has reached that point, you need to get professional help. . . . Perhaps my story will give someone in an abusive relationship—straight or gay—the courage to find help and get out. If you're in one now, get help now.

—GREG LOUGANIS
Diver

Take a Small Step Toward Familyhood

If you and your partner want to begin identifying yourselves as a couple but are not quite ready to take on insurance companies or wrestle with the IRS, try starting with these: Open a video membership together, list both of your names in the telephone book, or put both your names on the cat's veterinary records. Little actions—rarely met with homophobia—may help the two of you feel more like the couple that you are.

—CHRISTOPHER KEENAN
Children's Programming Executive

I love getting mail addressed to Mr. and Mr. Prince-MacNeil. It's the "Mr. and Mr." part I love. Our checking account has both of our names printed on the checks. When you get a statement from a multibillion-dollar bank or telephone company or whatever addressed to Mr. and Mr., it's very validating of the relationship.

—GREG PRINCE-MacNEIL
Chef

My husband and I keep a professional photo of the two of us on the mantelpiece. At first, I didn't want to do this. I thought it was cheesy—you know, two guys stuffed into suits and ties they never wear, with his hand resting on my shoulder to suggest this relaxed, poised look (which, of course, it doesn't). But Darren insisted. I still think the photo's cheesy, but I've grown to appreciate it. The act of having a professional studio portrait taken and displaying it in our home, despite the tackiness of the photo, adds to the strength of our union. People who visit us, including our families, take us more seriously because of that photo. I just wish the picture were a little better.

—HAL HORTON
Mechanic

Find Ways to Grow Together

In many straight relationships, children provide a powerful bond, something that both partners can focus their lives on together. The absence of children in a gay relationship can deprive the couple of glue. So couples must find ways to grow together—activities, projects, and goals that glue them together and give them a focus on the future.

—JOHN J. GANCAR II
Educator

Getting Hitched

Gay marriage is not a radical step; it is a profoundly humanizing, traditionalizing step. It is the first step in any resolution of the homosexual question—more important than any other institution, since it is the most central institution to the nature of the problem, which is to say, the emotional and sexual bond between one human being and another. If nothing else were done at all, and gay marriage were legalized, ninety percent of the political work necessary to achieve gay and lesbian equality would have been achieved. It is ultimately the only reform that truly matters.

—ANDREW SULLIVAN
Writer/Editor

Don't go calling every new boyfriend your husband. This denigrates the true meaning of the marriage commitment we are fighting for.

—RAY JACKSON
Graduate Student

If you think that gay and lesbian weddings are buying into a failed, patriarchal, heterosexual institution, then don't get married. But step out of the way of those of us who want it. Don't try to force your values on us. —THANE GUILDER

Husband-to-Be, as Soon as It's Legal

We already get married. Just keep on hitching up, going through the union ceremonies, and sooner or later the society and the law will catch up.

—JACKSON NGU

Married for Four Years

"*Changing the World*"

Save the Planet

I think the future of the world, the hope of the world, depends on us, that men who love men are the only people who can save the planet. That's our job, our purpose. We carry this other kind of energy that no one else carries, and it's entirely in our hands to save the world.

—ANDREW RAMER
Teacher/Writer

We have to realize that our loving each other is a good thing, not an unfortunate thing, and that we have a lot to teach straights about sex, love, strength and resistance.

—CARL WITTMAN
Writer

I like the idea of being a shepherd rather than the sheep. Leading the way for evolution, gay men are the beacons of the future. It is our responsibility to educate others about tolerance.

—JOHN FARNSWORTH
Banker/Poet

Simply by not breeding, you are making an important contribution to the environmental security of the planet. . . . You are not producing generations of energy-guzzling, resource-depleting, pollution-belching offspring. Put simply, that means Gay sex is the safest sex—for the whole world. . . . You're one of the best friends of the earth this planet has got.

—SIMON BIRCH
Writer

I would encourage the gay community to keep the pressure up but to do it with wisdom. See it as a long-term game. Give society a chance to come along rather than demanding they come along, since the price of demanding is going to cost the community in the long run.

—RAM DASS
Spiritual Activist/Author

A lot of gay people who might be reading this book at some point may be sitting alone in a room feeling very individual and isolated. It's important for them to accept their place in a movement and in a world. I really do believe that we as gay people have an involved role in the world. In helping. In being part of something greater than ourselves.

—MALCOLM BOYD
Author/Activist/Clergyman

What we do, each one of us, will reverberate through time long after we're gone. Our actions—or inactions—will influence what our people will have and be like fifty, five hundred, a thousand years from now. Do we want the gays of the future to go through the ordeals we did? We have responsibilities to the gays who will pass this way after us.

—MIKE VARADY
Writer/Activist

Liberate Your Soul

All people, but especially gay men at this moment in their collective development, need to awaken to the freedom of the inner world as much as the outer. For I believe that gay men and lesbians possess the ability to lead society's next phase of cultural revolution—liberation of the soul—if only they realize that potential.

—MARK THOMPSON
Writer

Developing a relationship with the inner Self is vitally important. To have that revolution go on in your own soul is much more profound than any revolution you can directly create around you in daily outer life. We'd make a lot more important progress with gay liberation in the outer world if more individual gays would wake up to this inner relationship.

—MITCH WALKER
Psychologist/Writer

Don't Get Discouraged

The space between Lincoln's signing the Emancipation Proclamation and the passage of the Civil Rights Act of 1964 was more than a century. I don't think it's going to take that long with gay rights, but it's important not to get carried away with either euphoria or despondency.

—GERRY STUDDS
Former U.S. Representative

We have to have the patience of Gandhi, the wisdom of King, and the militancy of Malcolm. I don't think it'll happen overnight. It will depend on the sacrifices we're willing to make. But by our sacrifices we will set ourselves free. My instincts tell me that we will do whatever it takes to be free. To go backward is unacceptable.

—DAVID MIXNER
Political Strategist

The inevitable part of pushing for significant change is that you lose early on. If you could win early on, it would mean that it wasn't a very big change. So, we lose. That's not bad. The losing is part of the price that you have to pay for eventually winning. The effects aren't good, but don't let them discourage us. This is a long-term battle.

—JOHN D'EMILIO

Professor, Author, and Director of the National Gay and Lesbian Task Force Policy Institute

Embrace Political Action

I continue to believe that any gay man or lesbian who does not oppose the prejudice and discrimination of organizations to which he or she may belong remains enslaved by the self-hatred such institutions engender. —RICHARD A. ISAY

Psychiatrist

You must be ready to assume responsibility because your given collective needs you and your vision, you and your secret shining ideas! —HARRY HAY

Queer Activist and Founding Father of Radical Faeries

If gays in America are ever to achieve equal rights, we must make it our business to overcome . . . this kind of lingering, often liberal discomfort, which—intentionally or not—insidiously demands that we know our place. Let's get out the word: Our place is wherever we want it to be. —BRUCE BAWER

Writer

The gay community has tended to fuse cultural self-expression with political tactics. For us, our right to offend people is a political statement. Unfortunately it's had a negative effect. Too much of our energy has gone into cultural self-expression, and not enough into conventional politics.

—BARNEY FRANK

U.S. Representative

I think everyone has the ability to be a community activist. . . . I do little seminars on how to fund-raise, and people always say, "I can't fund-raise." I say, "Yes, you can." Anyone can. Whether you've got $5 or $500,000 to give, stretch to whatever your stretch is. Then you will be doing your share for the community.

—CHUCK HOLMES

Porn Mogul

Always Vote

If gay and lesbian rights is your major issue, you have to follow what Samuel Gompers told workers: You reward your friends, and you punish your enemies. You vote for the people who are more supportive, and you vote against the people who are less supportive.

—BARNEY FRANK
U.S. Representative

We should endorse candidates, not parties. We have friends and enemies within both parties. We cannot be lazy voters. We must carefully choose who is worthy of our support.

—STEVE GUNDERSON
Former U.S. Representative

Small Acts of Revolution

Leave a gay magazine in your doctor's waiting lounge.

—NATHAN BLASINGAME
Restaurant Manager

Wipe phrases like "throws like a girl" out of your vocabulary.

—SAM WHITING
Actor Cum Activist

Every time we kiss/
we confirm the new world coming.

—ESSEX HEMPHILL
Poet

Stamp your money with gay slogans.

—LARRY ALDRICH
Happy-Go-Lucky Pedestrian

Use "gay" checks when paying bills. When you speak or write, use "I" or "us," not "they" or "them."

—MIKE VARADY
Writer/Activist

Take responsibility for your condoms. The gutter, alleys, under bushes, and so on, are not appropriate places to discard them.

—NICHOLAS BROAD
Educator

Go to your local jeweler with your lover to shop for matching rings—or earrings! . . .
Call him a him and her a her when talking about your love life. . . .
Send flowers to someone and don't use initials on the card.
Check into a hotel under Mr. and Mr. or Ms. and Ms. . . .
Be affectionate with your lover or partner upon arrival or departure at the airport.
Boycott a company or organization that discriminates against homosexuals, and *let them know about it!*

—HUMAN RIGHTS CAMPAIGN
"COMING OUT DAY" POSTER

Don't pay taxes. Give the money to drag queens for makeup instead.

—ROBERT L. RUCKER
Queer Poet

Our national gay rights groups are extraordinarily undersupported. Every gay man and lesbian in this country should join at least one national gay political group. If we all don't support our own political organizations, why should we expect other politicians to support us?

—KERRY INGRAM
Future Congressman

Be Courageous

It is courage that gets noticed, and courage that changes the world.

—ANDREW SULLIVAN
Writer/Editor

Great leaders of change have always met with disapproval and even outrage. Be willing to risk being unpopular in order to create a better world.

—JOSEPH HUNT
Artist/Writer/Songwriter

There's a transition that occurs when you go from your mind into more of the soul. For me, it happened after I banged my head against the wall one too many times. I finally reached a point where I said, "Fuck it, no more trusting the government. I'm not doing what's reasonable." And suddenly it becomes "By any means necessary."

—JOHN DURAN
Attorney/Activist

Fight Back

For Christ's sake, open your mouths; don't you people get tired of being stepped on?

—BETTE MIDLER
Honorary Fag

You have to take rights; they don't give them to you.

—NIGEL FINCH
Film Director

Declare your resistance from cradle to grave, and scream into the faces of oppression wherever you find them. Stand poised at every moment to punch, kick, bite, and burn your way to freedom. Pick fights with the enemy, then cheat, steal, lie, and sabotage to win. Revolt.

—ROBERT L. RUCKER
Queer Poet

The time for politeness has to end.

—DEREK JARMAN
Film Director

It's no longer an issue of whether to be in or out of the closet. If you're dead, you're dead. I really believe people out there are trying to kill me and my community. It's self-defense, my activism. It's how do you stay alive until Christmas?

—WADE RICHARDS
Activist

The only way we can win this battle is to out-love those who oppose us.

—MEL WHITE
Writer

Use Your Anger

It seems to me that rage is one of those two-sided powers: It can overpower you, or you can channel it until you are going across the sky like Apollo in his chariot.

—PAUL MONETTE
Writer

Being angry and hateful back is a weapon, a sword. But like a knight fighting a dragon, a big sword is not enough. To face the anger, ignorance, fear, and hatred of others and remain intact as a person takes honesty, bravery, courage, boldness, and love of self and others. Coming to terms with and being happy with one's sexual orientation in an environment that vilifies homosexuality is not for the cowardly.

—KARL DERRICK
Gardener/Property Manager

The question before each of us every day is where to direct our anger. When one is faced with life's crises, there are two possible responses: despair or determination. Despair often seems more logical. But determination is far more productive and usually far better for the soul.

—GERRY STUDDS
Former U.S. Representative

For all gay people, fighting hatred is a way to express the rage we may otherwise turn against ourselves. . . . Opposing discrimination in a prejudiced society is good for the psyche. It directs anger away from ourselves to where it rightfully belongs.

—RICHARD A. ISAY
Psychiatrist

Let Your Fantasies Give You Strength

I'm beginning to believe that one of the last frontiers left for radical gesture is the imagination. At least in my ungoverned imagination I can fuck somebody without a rubber, or I can, in the privacy of my own skull, douse Helms with a bucket of gasoline and set his putrid ass on fire or throw congressman William Dannemeyer off the empire state building. These fantasies give me distance from my outrage for a few seconds. They give me momentary comfort. Sexuality defined in images gives me comfort in a hostile world. They give me strength.

—DAVID WOJNAROWICZ
Writer/Performer

Consider tying a red ribbon around the throat of your least-favorite politician (e.g., Jesse Helms) until his eyes bulge and he turns blue.

—DAVID B. FEINBERG
Writer

I keep wishing that some group of men and women more courageous than I would start a terrorist group.

—LARRY KRAMER
Writer/Activist

I'm not from the school which says "We mustn't fight back and be just like they are." I'd *like* to kill somebody. I really would.

—DANIEL CURZON
Writer

Dreams Lead to Reality. Keep Dreaming.

Imagine no more poignant memorial services. No more “twentysomething and HIV-positive” support groups. No more AIDS protests, no more AIDS fund-raisers. *And no more fucking red ribbons.*

Imagine a future of equality, diversity, community. Imagine a time when gay men count gray hairs, not T-cells. Imagine a world where we’re raised to love ourselves as healthy, whole, and beautiful. *Imagine.*

Imagine a place where holding hands is not an act of courage, and having sex is not against the law. Imagine no more fear, no more grief.

Imagine no more new HIV infections.

—JOHN LEONARD
Seattle AIDS Educator and Community Activist

I thought if I ever could create a perfect world, I would want everyone to be equal. A world where the only rule would be respect, respect for each individual to live life the way he or she saw fit. A world where the only hate was directed toward hate. Remove the world's isms, and the ills would soon take leave. People would be judged as individuals and not in groups. Groups cause fears.

—E. LYNN HARRIS
Writer (from Just as I Am*)*

Don't Pass Your Pain On

We will not pass this pain on to the next generation of lesbians and gays. We will not leave this decade without our freedom. . . . We will not be silent gays and lesbians. We will be fighting lesbians and gays . . . we will be free.

—DAVID MIXNER
Political Strategist

Weep, if you must. Then go out and break some windows.

—ROBERT L. RUCKER
Queer Poet

Tell yourself: none of this ever had to happen. And then go make it stop. Whatever breath you have left. Grief is a sword or it is nothing.

—PAUL MONETTE
Writer

It's Time to Be Free

Take your place in the sun, 'cause the war has been won. Ain't no stoppin' us now. All God's children are free!

—RUPAUL
Entertainer (from "Free to Be")

Our suffering has not defeated us—it has galvanized us and strengthened our resolve to be free. We have so many talents, so much intelligence, love, and courage to bring this troubled nation. If it embraces us, it will be a stronger and more beautiful place. But until that time of freedom arrives, we have no choice but to continue through non-violent action to fight vigorously for what is right. No community is more determined than this one to come out of the darkness and seize the protection and freedom guaranteed to it by the Constitution of the United States of America.

—DAVID MIXNER
Political Strategist

Forgive

When we fags and dykes rule the world, which is of course coming at the beginning of the new millennium, be gracious enough to forgive the straights for all the awful things they've done to us.

—AARON PEOPLES
Optimist

Put this book aside and love. May you of a better future, love without a care and remember we loved too. As the shadows closed in, the stars came out.

—DEREK JARMAN
Film Director

Acknowledgments

Besides the hundreds of men represented in this volume, there are thousands more who shared their thoughts and feelings with me to be considered for inclusion in this book. Many heartfelt thanks to all these men who believed in and supported *Speaking Out*.

Thanks to those who hosted the focus groups and workshops in which some of this book's material was derived: Eric Raptosh, Greg Albey, Dave Black, C. J. Morritz, Dwight Stevens, Craig Scott, Sam Whiting, David Fischer, the University of Washington Gay, Lesbian and Bisexual Association, Lambert House, and Queercore at Gay City.

Thanks to Kaley Davis and Eric Raptosh for their computer and Internet guidance.

While most of the material in this volume was written directly for *Speaking Out*, some of the quotes are from previously published sources. For the use of extended quotations, I gratefully acknowledge the following authors, publications, and/or publishers:

Pages 19, 170, 174: Barney Frank, Gerry Studds from "The Boys in the Band," *The Advocate,* October 17, 1995, pages 40–46. Reprinted from *The Advocate.* Used with permission. Pages 135, 142, 143: Edmund White, Larry Kramer, Christopher Isherwood, from

The Advocate, August 23, 1994, pages 78–80. Reprinted from *The Advocate.* Used with permission.

Amy Appleby, editor, *Quentin Crisp's Book of Quotations,* Macmillan, 1989. W. H. Auden, *About the House,* Random House, 1965. James Baldwin, *Giovanni's Room,* Dial Press, 1956. David Blanton, *Queer Notions,* Running Press, 1996. Frank Browning, *A Queer Geography,* Crown, 1996. Martin Duberman, *Cures: A Gay Man's Odyssey,* Dutton, 1991. Martin Duberman, *Midlife Queer,* Scribner, 1996. David B. Feinberg, *Eighty-Sixed,* Viking, 1989. David B. Feinberg, *Queer and Loathing,* Viking, 1994. Harvey Fierstein, *Torch Song Trilogy,* Gay Presses of New York, 1981. Gregory Flood, *I'm Looking for Mr. Right but I'll Settle for Mr. Right Away,* Brob House, 1986. Charles Flowers, editor, *Out, Loud, and Laughing,* Anchor Books, 1995. Keith Haring, *Journals,* Viking, 1996. E. Lynn Harris, *Just As I Am,* Doubleday, 1994. Essex Hemphill, *Tongues Untied,* Gay Men's Press, 1987. David Herbert, *Relations and Revelations,* Peter Owens Publishers (London), 1992. Richard Isay, *Becoming Gay,* Pantheon, 1996. Rod and Bob Jackson-Paris, *Straight from the Heart,* Warner Books, 1994. Derek Jarman, *At Your Own Risk,* The Overlook Press, 1992. Ed Karvoski, Jr., editor, *A Funny Time to Be Gay,* Fireside, 1997. Larry Kramer, *The Normal Heart,* New American Library, 1985. Tony Kushner, *Angels in America*

Part One: Millennium Approaches, Theatre Communications Group, 1993. Simon LeVay, *Queer Science,* The MIT Press, 1996. Marvin Liebman, *Coming Out Conservative,* Chronicle Books, 1992. David Loovis, *Gay Spirit: A Guide to Becoming a Sensuous Homosexual,* A Strawberry Hill Book/Grove Press, 1974. Greg Louganis, *Breaking the Surface,* Random House, 1995. David Mixner, *Stranger Among Friends,* Bantam, 1996. Ethan Mordden, *How Long Has This Been Going On?,* Villard, 1994. Walt Odets, *In the Shadow of the Epidemic,* Duke University Press, 1995. Joe Orton, *The Orton Diaries,* HarperCollins, 1988. Robert Rodi, *Kept Boy,* Dutton, 1996. Paul Rudnick, *Jeffrey,* Plume, 1994. Leigh Rutledge, *Unnatural Quotations,* Alyson Publications, 1988. Douglas Sadownick, *Sex Between Men,* HarperSanFrancisco, 1996. Michelangelo Signorile, *Outing Yourself,* Random House, 1995. Andrew Sullivan, *Virtually Normal,* Knopf, 1995. R. G. Talbert, *Warts and All,* Rain City Publishers. Mark Thompson, *Gay Soul: Finding the Heart of Gay Spirit and Nature,* HarperSanFrancisco, 1994. Andy Warhol, *The Philosophy of Andy Warhol,* Harcourt Brace Jovanovich, 1975. Jon Winokur, *A Curmudgeon's Garden of Love,* New American Library, 1989. Karl Wittman, "Refugees from Amerika" in *The Homosexual Dialectic* (Joseph McCaffrey, editor), Prentice-Hall, 1972. David Wojnarowicz, *Close to the Knives: A Memoir of Disintegration,* Vintage, 1991.